GHOST CHAMBER

Celia Rees

Hodder Children's Books

a division of Hachette Children's Books

Also by Celia Rees

City of Shadows
A Trap in Time
The Host Rides Out

Soul Taker

For Terry — my 'researcher'

NOTE FROM THE AUTHOR

'I am drawn to mysteries and, judging from the success of Dan Brown's *Da Vinci Code*, I'm not alone in this. Few organisations are more mysterious than the Knights Templar: the secretive order of warrior monks who gained fabulous wealth and power before being suppressed amid accusations of witchcraft and heresy. Knights Templar possessions included the small village of Temple Balsall in Warwickshire. When I was a child, my family attended Christmas Eve services there in the plain Templar church.

Temple Balsall is en route from where I live now to my family home. Taking that journey one day, I saw the little church half hidden by the trees and I began to speculate. The Templar treasure, never found, was rumoured to have included ritual objects of immense occult power. What if they had found their way here? A village so small, so obscure, would be the perfect hiding place . . .

Further on, I passed an old inn undergoing conversion into a private house. I love real ghost stories and knew that some of the most haunted sites in England are hotels and public houses. What if this inn had once been the preceptory, the Templars' dwelling place? The use of a building might change, but psychic presences remain, good or bad. What would it be like to live there? Sometimes home is the scariest place to be . . .'

Celia Rees has written many books for children and teenagers, including the *City of Shadows* trilogy and *Soul Taker*. *Witch Child*, *Sorceress* and *Pirates!* were short listed respectively for the Guardian Children's Fiction, Whitbread and W.H. Smith Awards. Her latest novel is *The Wish House*, published by Macmillan.

Celia Rees lives in Leamington Spa Warwickshire, with husband. She has one daughter, Catrin, who now lives in London.

First published in Great Britain in 1997
by Hodder Children's Books

This edition published 2007
by Hodder Children's Books

4

A Catalogue record for this book is available from the British Library

ISBN-10: 0 340 93202 3
ISBN-13: 978034093202 3

Typeset in Bembo by Avon DataSet Ltd,
Bidford-on-Avon, Warwickshire

Printed in the UK by CPI Bookmarque, Croydon, CR0 4TD

The paper and board used in this paperback by Hodder Children's Books
are natural recyclable products made from wood grown in sustainable
forests. The manufacturing processes conform to the environmental
regulations of the country of origin.

Hodder Children's Books
a division of Hachette Children's Books
338 Euston Road, London NW1 3BH
An Hachette Livre UK company

PREFACE

Year – 1310
Place – The preceptory of the Knights Templar, Temple Marton, England

Stephen de Banville was alone. His brother knights arrested, he himself declared apostate, a fugitive, excommunicate. In France, members of the Brotherhood had been tried, tortured and put to the stake.

He had remained, a great and sacred trust put upon him, because of his skill in working with stone. His Order, the Poor Knights of the Temple of Solomon, had been one of the richest in the whole of Christendom, owning legendary treasures, the Shroud of Christ, shards of the True Cross, the Holy Grail.

Their most venerated relic, the secrets of secrets, had never been seen outside the Brotherhood, but tales of its power were legion. Many had died to protect it, were dying now, accused of terrible practices – devil worship, black magic – the flesh torn from their bones in hideous torture until the fires of the Inquisition brought merciful release. They died protesting innocence, denying that such a thing existed; it was mere rumour made up by those jealous of Templar power. Stephen himself had believed this, believed the accusations to be foul lies, felt that he and his Order served Christ truly. Until now.

The relic, the secret of secrets, was here, in Temple Marton. Knights, with faces burnt black by the sun of the Holy Land, had smuggled it out of France from under the grasping hand of a King who wished to use it for his own ends.

Temple Marton was small, obscure, cut off by water and forest. That is why it had been chosen. Stephen's task was to build a shrine, seal in the relic of relics. His task done, what would he do now? Give himself up? Join his Brothers in prison? Flee? Put off his distinctive habit, shave his beard, grow his hair, exchange sword for plough and become a peasant?

He would do none of these things. He had seen inside the mysterious casket. No one must know of its existence; no soul must ever see it. The contents were an offence against God and man, the worst kind of abomination. The object was truly evil. It possessed a power that would be sought and fought over endlessly. There would always be those who would desire it, seeking to bind it to them, to make it serve their own ends, to wield for themselves the forces it contained. Released into the world, it would wreak havoc, bringing death and destruction to innocent and guilty, unleashing a tide of blood to sweep on from generation to generation, down through the centuries.

He had thought to destroy it, but it was bound with spells that only a Magister could penetrate. He did not possess that kind of ability; his skill was in his hands. There lay his solution. He smoothed the wall he had just completed, picked up chisel, square and mallet, and began to work, shaping and placing, stone upon stone, walling himself in.

Alive . . .

1

'Do you believe in ghosts?'

Hugh Goodman leaned close in the back of the car, whispering the words right into Bethan's ear. He jogged his sister's shoulder when she did not respond, and asked once more in the same insistent creepy voice, the voice he kept for scaring her. 'Do you, Bethan? Do you?'

'No,' she answered, and then added 'not really' because, when you are seven, you can never be a hundred per cent sure.

'Why do you read those, then?' He pointed to the book on her lap. *Prepare to be Scared – to Death!* Silvery letters slithered a warning over the lurid-green shapeless mass creeping across the cover.

'Reading's different. You don't have to believe in it.' Her eyes turned back to the page she was on but he nudged her again. 'Leave me alone.' She pulled away, burrowing into her own corner. 'Stop bugging me or I'll tell Mum.'

'I just wanted to know.' She could hear his grin, she did not need to see him. 'I just wanted to know if you did or not, because . . .'

Bethan scowled. 'Because what?'

'Can you two stop squabbling, for goodness sake.' Their mother's voice came from the driver's seat. 'We're here now.'

They all looked out as the car came to a halt. Bethan's grey eyes widened in disbelief. This was to be their home for two whole weeks.

The building was old, so old that it lacked the squared edges of modern buildings. The walls bulged at odd angles between huge timbers which retained the curves and bends of forest trees. Gables, set into the roof, jutted out to shadow a crooked line of leaded windows. Old glass in the little panes reflected the summer sun unevenly; some glittered bright, some absorbed light, as though each black peeling frame contained an untried crossword puzzle. At the base of the walls, whitewash crumbled to reveal powdery grey stone. The whole place was like something out of a fairytale, as if it had always been there, as if it had never been built at all, as if it had just grown.

'Are you sure this is the right place?' Bethan asked, hoping Mum had made a mistake.

'Of course I am!' Her mother glanced at the instructions taped to the dashboard. 'Saracen's Head, Temple Marton. There can hardly be two pubs with that name in a village this size.'

It wasn't a pub any more, the board had been removed from the high crosspiece, the chains hung creaking like an empty gibbet. Peeling letters on the dingy walls spelt *Saracen's Head*. Next to the name, in ghostly faded outline, was the word *Hotel*.

'Is this the place Dad's bought?' Bethan stared, appalled.

'Yes.' Her mother sighed. 'Although God knows how he

2

got a mortgage *or* anyone stupid enough to insure it. Stay here,' she got out of the car, 'all of you. I'm going to find him.'

Janet Goodman slammed the door, her frown deepening. When Philip, her estranged husband, had told her he was buying a house, she had been glad to hear it. He had moved out two years ago this September; it was about time he settled down and took on his proper share of caring for the children. She looked up at the building with its cracking plaster and bleached half-timbering. Trust him to buy a ruin. When she had asked him to take the kids for two weeks in the summer because she had a holiday planned, he had sounded less than enthusiastic.

'Normally I'd love to, of course, no problem,' he'd said, in reply to her request. 'It's just that, at the moment, things are a bit chaotic, what with the renovation work—'

At the time, she had dismissed his reluctance as selfish shilly-shallying, but maybe he had a point. It looked like they were rebuilding the house from the inside out. A faint misgiving started up, but she dismissed it. She wasn't going to back down, cancel the holiday, take the kids away again. If he thought that, he had another think coming.

With his mother safely out of the way, Hugh pointed up at the ancient facade, ready to exploit his sister's deepening alarm.

'Sure you don't believe in ghosts, Bethan? Because I bet there are hundreds in there, ghouls too. Thousands, even.'

'I don't like it.' Bethan stuck out her lower lip. 'I want Mum to come back. I want to go with her. I don't want to stay here . . .'

'Well, you've got to.' Sally Goodman turned from the seat in front. 'We've got to stay for a while with Dad. Mum's going on holiday with her new friend, you know that.' She removed her sunglasses and smiled. 'It'll be OK, Beth.'

Bethan looked up, eyes wide and doubtful. Curls of dark hair framed her delicate elfin face. Sometimes she looked younger than seven.

'It'll be fun,' Sally added, sounding more certain than she felt. 'You'll see.'

Bethan's thumb crept into her mouth and she settled back into her seat, not entirely convinced.

'Don't wind her up, Hugh. We can do without that.' Sally's tone hardened as she addressed her brother.

'It was only a joke!' Hugh's answer came back, his voice breaking and sulky.

'Not funny.'

'I'm going to have a look round,' he said, opening the car door.

'Mum said—'

'I'm only going round the back. I'm bursting for a pee.' Hugh flicked back a lock of sandy hair and fixed her with a defiant stare and then went off, hands thrust deep in the pockets of his baggy jeans. As he walked away, he put in a do-what-I-like swagger, knowing Sally would be watching

4

him. He was going on thirteen, nearly as tall as her now, and not a kid any more. Just because she was three years older, he didn't have to take her orders.

Sally stared after him while her sister muttered to her army of stuffed toys in the back of the car. Bethan could not understand why Mum would want to go away and not take them, and she didn't like Roger, Mum's new 'friend'. She wasn't alone in that; *none* of them did. Sally folded her arms and closed her eyes. Their fortnight stay here was already threatening to turn into a nightmare and it was only just beginning.

When her parents split up, Sally, Hugh and Bethan had stayed with their mother in a town just north of London, many kilometres from this West Country backwater.

Just after Dad moved out, Sally remembered Bethan asking their mum, in the way only five-year-olds can, 'Why don't you like Daddy any more?'

'I do,' her mother had replied, tears clouding her eyes. 'I just can't live with him and keep my sanity.'

Philip Goodman, their father, was a writer of popular stories, exploring mysteries that had puzzled scholars for centuries. His books were the most important thing in his life and each one could take years to write, containing endless hours of work and painstaking research. His efforts did not go unrewarded. He was very successful, his books rode high in the bestseller lists, but that was not why he did it. His enthusiasm for each one bordered on obsession.

That was one of the reasons for the marriage break-up.

Philip travelled a lot, often abroad, and was gone for months at a time – these frequent absences had been another source of friction within the marriage. His foreign trips increased after the separation and, when he was in England, he spent his days in libraries and his nights working on the computer. He lived where his studies took him; in rented accommodation, cramped rooms crammed with books, and with little space for visiting children.

He came to see them instead, often appearing unannounced (Philip liked surprises). Sally's mother said he did it deliberately to drive her crazy, but the children did not care, just as long as he was there. He would shower them with presents and whisk them off for treats. He generally thought up some pretty wild things to do: hot-air ballooning, powerboat riding, flying in a helicopter.

He would drop them back at the end of a frantic day, exchange a few words with their mother and disappear again with a cheery wave. They never knew when they would see him again. This was not because he didn't care, or didn't love them; he often did not know where he would be from one month to the next himself. He had seemed content to live a roaming, semi-nomadic existence . . . and then suddenly he had bought this place.

'I'm hot,' Bethan complained, cutting into Sally's thoughts. 'Where's Mum?'

'I'll go and find out.' Sally opened her door.

'Can I come?'

'Better not,' Sally said. They might be arguing and that would upset her. 'Why don't you go and look for Hugh? See what he's up to?'

'Where is he?'

'He's round there poking about.' Sally indicated an area at the side of the house.

'What's he doing?'

'I don't know. Go and see.'

Sally made her way over to the house. There was no sound, no one about. If it wasn't for an overturned wheelbarrow, and a cement-encrusted mixer, she would have thought the place deserted. The house itself had a neglected atmosphere, as though no one lived there. Sally caught the twitch of a curtain pulled back, the smudge of a white face looking out. It must be a workman, she told herself, but the face had seemed too old for that. It looked like an old man dressed in black . . .

A drill started up, jolting Sally back to reality, whining a welcome as she walked up the dusty plank path to the door. Someone is very keen to keep the evil spirits out, she thought, as she ducked her head to enter. The horseshoe above the portal had been hammered in so hard it was now part of the lintel.

'What have you got there?' Bethan asked as she came up behind her brother.

Hugh was squatting down by the wall, holding

something, arms wide. Bethan hung back slightly. He had changed lately, his moods becoming less certain. He often ignored her, didn't even bother to tease her much any more, let alone play. But things might be different now they were on holiday.

Hugh pushed back his long fringe and reached towards his find. 'Look what I've got. Isn't it great?'

Bethan glanced over his shoulder and met the gaze of a ferocious painted face. A richly coloured turban swirled above crinkling eyes. Whites gleamed against swarthy skin and pupils showed so black they looked drilled out. Thin lines of beard and moustache, the glossy blue and green of a raven's wing, showed below the hooked nose and framed red lips stretched back over pointed teeth. A jewel glowed in one ear. A brown hand, encrusted in rings, clutched a wide and wicked-looking scimitar. Behind him a sandy desert landscape swept away, dotted with dunes and tiny pyramids, blurring into infinity.

'Err . . .' Bethan's snub nose wrinkled. 'What is it?'

'It's the Saracen's Head. The inn sign. What do you *think* it is? It must have been left here when they took it down.'

'I don't like it,' Bethan said quietly, her thumb creeping into her mouth, as it often did when she was worried or frightened.

'No one is asking you to. It's a great find and I'm having it, not you.'

'I don't want it, so there. I don't like it,' the little girl said again.

'Why not? It's only a picture. You are *so* stupid!'

'Just don't. That's all. It's nasty.'

Bethan could not explain her instinctive dislike of the sign Hugh had been so excited to find. 'Creepy' wasn't a strong enough word, and 'malevolent' had yet to enter her vocabulary. All she knew was that the Saracen's eyes could follow you about. She could feel them, peering through the weeds. And there was something else. A head was all it was. She looked carefully: there was no neck, just a gap. The Saracen's head had been cut off from its body.

'I don't want it near me,' she added, voice muffled by her thumb. 'Leave it where it is, Hugh.'

'No way,' Hugh replied irritably. She was beginning to get on his nerves now. 'It's going in *my* room. Why don't you go and find Sally?'

Bethan took the hint and left Hugh frowning down at the sign, figuring out how to move it. It was heavy, much heavier than it looked. Hugh went to pick it up, and had to let it slip back down. He would not be able to shift it by himself.

'Need a hand?'

Hugh turned to find a man standing behind him. He thought at first that he might be one of the workmen, but his clothes were not right for that. He was wearing dark slacks and a leather jacket. Hugh smiled uncertainly, and the man smiled back, thin lips retracting to show a gap between his front teeth and a gold cap.

9

'Name's Garvin. Mark Garvin.' The smile creased his face but did not quite make it to his colourless eyes. 'Haven't seen you before. You new round here?'

'Yes. My name's Hugh Goodman.' Hugh shook the man's thin, hard hand. 'My dad owns this place.'

'Oh.' The pale eyes flickered interest. 'That right? Didn't know he had kids.' His hand went to his head, smoothing down a few thin strands. What was left of his greying hair was pulled back into a ponytail. 'You staying with him?'

'Yes, as it happens. We've just arrived.'

'We?'

'My sisters and I.'

'What about Mum?'

'She's separated from my dad . . .'

Garvin sensed an edge of hostility and changed tack.

'Staying long?' he asked, careful to keep his tone conversational.

'A couple of weeks . . .' Hugh nearly added, 'What's it to you?' He didn't like being quizzed by nosy strangers and the man's cheesy grin was starting to annoy him, but he remembered Mum's lecture about being friendly to the 'natives' and swallowed the words.

'You should enjoy it. Interesting village, and this place,' Garvin glanced up at the pub, 'has quite a history. Get your dad to tell you about it.'

'Do you live round here?'

'Nah.' The man shook his head. 'Just visiting like

yourself. Like I said, it's an interesting place.' He nodded towards the sign. 'Sure you don't want help with this?'

'Yes, I'm sure. It's all right. Thank you.'

Hugh grabbed the sign, determined to lift it on his own, but again it slipped. It slid down through his hands and he felt something, a small nail perhaps, furrow the flesh of his palm. The gash was deep, filling quickly and overflowing until crimson splashed down the face on the painted sign.

Hugh pulled his hand away, ignoring the pain, more concerned about making a mess. He need not have worried: the dripped blood was already drying in the hot sun, mixing and merging with the complex hues that made up the coppery face and red-lipped mouth. Hugh's blood was now part of the painting.

'Ouch!' The man mimed sympathy. 'You'd better get that seen to.'

'Yes. Good idea.'

'Be seeing you!'

He smiled his thin-lipped lizard smile at the boy's retreating back. It was also time for him to go: he had to report the arrival of Philip Goodman's family to Mr Holt. The Saracen's Head was the focus of some very special attention; anything to do with the former public house was of particular interest to his friend and companion. Mr Holt was a person with very unusual powers, so these children turning up might well have been predicted. Not that it would make any difference. The Great Work would go on, whatever occurred. Mr Holt was about as ruthless and determined a man as it was possible to meet, and nothing – but nothing – could interfere with one of his projects.

2

Sally paused to allow her eyes to adjust to the dimness inside the house. The downstairs was being taken apart; all the bar room fittings were being ripped out. Huge stone slabs stood on end where the floor was being re-flagged. She hesitated, trying to plan a route through the mess, when a young man stepped out from just inside the door. He moved his face mask and set down his power drill.

'Hi. I'm Will. Will Harding.' He extended his hand to her. 'You must be Sally.'

The girl standing in front of him was tall, slim and pretty, with shoulder-length blonde hair and large blue eyes, set wide, in a face both strong and delicate at the same time.

'Pleased to meet you.' Sally shook his hand, and laughed. 'I thought the place was deserted, like the *Marie Celeste*, until I saw a face upstairs, and then I heard your drill—'

'Upstairs?' Will frowned. 'Didn't know there was anyone up there; I thought everyone was on dinner break.' Then his brow cleared. 'Oh, I expect you saw Gran; she's probably getting your rooms ready.'

'Your gran?' It was Sally's turn to frown. 'It looked more like a man . . .' She shook her head. 'It doesn't matter.'

'If you're looking for your dad, he's out back. Across the

yard. Just go through, but stay on the planks.'

Sally thanked him. He was maybe a year or two older than her. Brown eyes, very dark, smiled from a white clown mask of plaster dust which hid the rest of his face, making it difficult to see what he really looked like, or how old he was.

Sally picked her way out to a cobbled yard containing weathered picnic benches left over from when it had been a beer garden. Rear access was through an archway wide enough to take a coach and horses; otherwise the space was enclosed by the wings of the house and a series of outhouses. One of these had been converted into a study. The door was shut, but spaces between the planks meant arguing voices were finding their way out. Sally found herself listening. She couldn't help it.

'Your work!' Her mother's voice rang out, high and angry. 'It's always your work. I thought it might be different now you've got your own place, but all you ever think about is yourself. How long is it? Nearly two years? I have them day in, day out. And all you can manage is a couple of visits.'

'I've been busy—'

'Well, so have I,' her mother's voice cut in again. 'And I'm taking a holiday.'

'With him, I suppose.'

That was a reference to Roger. Janet Goodman was still young and attractive, entitled to some kind of life of her own. Sally could respect that, and she admired the way her mother had picked up the threads of her former career after Philip left. Money was not a problem, Philip made sure of that, but Mum had taken courses to update her skills and had joined a design firm. That's where Roger came on the scene. He was a senior partner.

Sally was not sure whether this holiday Mum had planned with him marked the beginning of a serious relationship, or whether it was a gesture to spite Philip. If that was her plan, it was succeeding: her father sounded unhappy, emphasising 'him', unable to keep the jealousy out of his voice.

'Yes, with *him*.' Her mother stressed the word, too, digging it in. 'Not that it is any of your business.'

'Now is not a terrific time. You've seen the state of the place and I'm just about to start on a new book . . .'

'Tough. They are here now and here they stay. A fortnight is not too much to ask, surely to God?'

'It's just this particular fortnight. I've got to go away for a while.'

'When?'

'In a couple of days.'

'Cancel it.'

'I can't, Janet. Be reasonable.'

'Put it off.'

'It's not just one thing. I have a series of meetings, and it's taken me ages to set them up. I've got to go to my publishers, and British Heritage; I'm seeking permission and funding to excavate. I'm also meeting Clive Rowlands, he's heading the archaeological team who will be doing the excavation—'

'You *knew* the children were coming and you arrange meetings?' her mother's voice shouted, incredulous. 'And what excavation? Are you going off on a dig or something?'

'No. I'm staying right here. This is the place I want to excavate.'

'What on earth for? As if it wasn't enough of a mess without archaeologists tramping all over the place. I don't believe it!'

'That's what I mean,' her father sighed. 'That's why it's not a good time for the kids to be here, don't you see?'

'No. I don't see. And I don't understand why you want it excavated. Who ever heard of a pub being excavated?'

'This is not just any old pub. It's a Knights Templar preceptory, I'm pretty sure of it.' Excitement crept into his voice as he tried to explain. 'I want to prove it; so little is known about them. Who knows what might be discovered here? This could be an important site—'

'Save it for your readers, Philip,' her mother cut in. 'You'll just have to cope. I've got a plane to catch and I intend to be on it.'

Mum had the final word, as she usually did, and now the study was quiet. Sally could imagine them looking at each other, stunned and baffled, like they couldn't understand how they'd ever got into this position. They were like two soldiers peering across a no-man's-land they had created themselves. They needed to sit down and talk, not shout and hurl accusations, but they did not seem to be able to speak for two minutes together without one of them goading the other into a rage.

'I want to see Dad!' Bethan came hurtling into the yard. 'Where is he?'

'He's in there, with Mum.' Sally pointed towards the study. 'But I don't think it would be a very good idea . . .'

'Dad! Dad!' Bethan called out and ran for the door, completely ignoring what she had just been told.

'What have you done to your hand?' Sally asked, when Hugh came through. Blood was oozing through the knuckles.

'I just caught it on something.'

'Let's see.'

'No. It's nothing. Don't fuss.'

'Here.' Sally gave him a tissue to staunch the bleeding.

'OK. Thanks.' Hugh hid his hand in his pocket as his father came out bearing Bethan on his shoulder.

'Hello you two!'

He looked pale, Sally thought, as he came over to greet her and Hugh. He had lost a bit of weight and the tan he'd got from time spent abroad was fading from his face. His hair needed cutting and streaks of grey were appearing here and there. He looked older than the last time she'd seen him, and more strained.

'Sally! How are you?' His blue eyes, a shade or two lighter than her own, crinkled at the corners, smiling

17

down. 'And Hugh, how are you doing?' He put an arm round each of them. 'I've been so looking forward to you coming to stay.' The words that were not quite true came with a little extra squeeze to the shoulder. 'Place is a mess, I'm afraid – it'll be a bit like camping out – but it could be fun. What do you say?' Before they could reply, he glanced over at his wife, standing slightly apart, looking at her watch. 'I've been telling your mother. Haven't I, Janet?'

Janet Goodman nodded slightly but otherwise her small, fine-featured face remained impassive. She pushed at her short dark hair and looked at her watch again, pulling at the simple linen dress she had chosen for travelling, straightening herself for departure. She was moving away, her mind at the airport already.

'You're going to like it here, I know . . .' As Philip Goodman spoke, a cloud suddenly obscured the sun and a cold little wind sneaked round the yard, stirring up dust, whirling up litter and empty crisp packets. Sally shivered, gooseflesh creeping up her arms. It looked an interesting place all right, but how did Dad know they were going to like it?

3

Janet Goodman drove off, leaving the scent of her light
summer perfume, a cloud of dust – and her husband in
charge of his family. The children took the luggage up to
their rooms, but had no time to unpack or settle in. Their
father wanted to show them round first, give them a
guided tour of the house.

They visited every room, barring the cellar and the attic.
The ground floor looked like a building site and still held
traces of its former life. The bar and seating had been taken
out, but the room retained the faint smell of beer and
cigarettes, and what remained of the plaster was varnished
brown by tobacco. The central pillars had little shelves and
a selection of stained beer mats.

The building work was being done by Jack Harding &
Co., the firm run by Will's father. Jack Harding was a big
friendly man with a ready laugh, wide shoulders and a
thatch of fair hair. A grin split his broad pleasant face when
Philip introduced the children, and he held out his large
hand to bid them welcome. His palm was so scarred and
calloused, his handshake felt like a fistful of cockleshells.

Sally was relieved to find that the upper storey had yet
to be affected by the confusion below. It was still like a
small country hotel. There was even a TV lounge and they

each had their own room, aired and prepared by Will's grandmother, who seemed to be acting as a kind of housekeeper.

Edna Harding was a thin, small woman, with a sharp-featured face, a handshake as firm as her son's, and a brisk no-nonsense manner. She had a neat bandage on Hugh's hand within two minutes of meeting him: she scolded him for making a mess of himself, and Philip for not noticing, but her dark eyes were kind, and her touch gentle.

She wished them welcome and had obviously done her best to make them comfortable. Each room had fresh flowers and, even though the furnishings were worn, the surfaces were highly polished, the bed-linen starched and spotless.

Bethan took to Mrs Harding immediately and went off with her to the kitchen while Philip talked to his other two children. He wanted them to understand the historical importance of the place, the reason why he bought it.

Sally looked round; some of her father's enthusiasm about living there began to rub off on her. The building was very old. Sally couldn't recall ever having been in a place as old before. Anywhere you didn't have to pay to go in, or wasn't a ruin. Some of the oak had come from trees felled between 1121 and 1225. She ran a finger along the whorls and gnarled contours. It was like touching living history; who would not be impressed and awed by it? Most of the great beams were encased in plaster now, the interior had been modelled and remodelled around them, but they were still there, supporting the building, giving it shape and meaning, keeping the past alive inside the present.

Her father was determined to uncover the past, restore the building's original features. Most of all, he wanted to prove his theory; that this was the preceptory, the communal dwelling place used by the Knights Templar.

'I can explain more, if you'd like me to—'

Sally and Hugh nodded, his enthusiasm was infectious. Philip smiled: even if his work left his wife cold, Sally and Hugh were old enough to make up their own minds whether they wanted to share in his projects.

'OK, then.' Philip Goodman rubbed his hands. 'Why don't I see if I can rustle up some tea? We can take it over to the study.'

Hugh followed his father and Sally, his excitement mounting. He was really glad they had come now. Not just to see Dad, although he was pleased about that: he had missed his father a lot in the last two years and visits never seemed to go right. Like songs out of rhyme, they began tense and awkward and, just when they were beginning to get natural, to pick up the old rhythm, Philip dumped them back. Dad was more relaxed here, especially now Mum had gone – less on his best behaviour.

It was a brilliant place, just right for Dad. In fact, it was one of the most interesting buildings Hugh had ever been in. Not just the history, although that was intriguing enough, but it had enormous discovery potential. Hugh was a great collector, and relished finding things, but what could you find in a modern house? Hugh had lived in one all his life and never found a thing. It was different here. He'd already made two finds and they had only just arrived! The sign outside and now— His fingers closed over a stone, flat and round, a fossil of some kind, an ammonite. He had spotted it from the stairs, lodged on top of the lintel. It seemed a shame to leave it gathering dust. Dangerous, too. With all the work going on, someone might have thrown it out. It would be safer with Hugh. For the moment, his trouser pocket would provide sanctuary.

Their father's study was quiet and cool. The white stone walls gave off the tang of fresh emulsion.

Charts, maps, photographs and photocopies – Blu-Tacked up in interleaving layers – stirred and subsided as the door opened and closed. They were all related to his current project: the Knights Templar. The Poor Knights of the Temple of Solomon. An order of soldier monks, set up at the time of the Crusades to protect pilgrims from the Saracens.

They got their name, Philip explained, from their headquarters which had been in the Temple of Solomon in Jerusalem. An enlarged photo of a stained-glass window showed a Knight kneeling in prayer, his chain-mailed arms reaching up in supplication, his white cloak, emblazoned on the shoulder with a splayed red cross, draped over shining armour. The white mantle symbolized chastity, the distinctive red cross showed that they were warriors of Christ.

'The arms of the cross are of equal length, wider at the ends than at the centre. It became their emblem, recognized everywhere. The Templars were highly effective soldiers, fearless in battle. The *Croix Patte* was respected by all, even Saladin. They became rich and powerful with a string of castles in the Holy Land, many of which still stand, and estates and property all over Europe.'

Hugh and Sally listened, spellbound, as their father talked on, describing the Knights' exploits in the Crusades, the battles and sieges in the Holy War against Muslim hordes determined to oust them from the land the Templars called Outremer, the land across the sea. The way he told it was not like history at all. He made these medieval knights sound like a cross between the SAS and the French Foreign Legion.

The Templars lived by The Rule, which controlled every aspect of their lives down to what they ate and how they dressed. The Order was an organisation with complex chains of command and vows of absolute loyalty, oaths reinforced by secret ceremonies. To betray – or disobey – meant death. Glamour and mystery surrounded the Templars, feeding legend and medieval romance, making them into King Arthur's Grail Knights, turning them into myth.

'Didn't something awful happen to them?' Sally frowned, searching her memory.

'Yes. The Order was disbanded, its wealth and property plundered, and many of its members were burnt at the stake. That shows the fate of the last Grand Master, Jacques de Molay.'

Philip pointed to a coloured illustration of an execution. Red flames licking round two men, tonsured, naked except for loincloths, bound back to back to a wooden stake. The execution took place on an island in the Seine. The medieval painting made the dying men look huge, the island too small to support them; the city walls, along the opposite bank, were shorter than the spectators drawn to watch. The artist may not have mastered perspective but had accurately recorded the shimmer of the fierce heat, the distorting agony on their faces. The man nearest to the victims held his arm up to protect his own face as he stoked the flames with a long pole.

'But why?' Sally asked, suppressing a shudder.

'They became too powerful, particularly in France. Powerful enough to earn the enmity of the King, Philip the Fair. He turned on them and, in 1307, had them all arrested.'

Sally looked up at the figures cringing in the circling flames. 'They must have done more than that to deserve such terrible deaths.'

'Some say no. Others . . .' He paused. 'Others thought their end was nothing more or less than they deserved, given the nature of the crimes they were supposed to have committed.'

'What crimes?'

'Heresy, unnatural practices, witchcraft and sorcery. You name it; including idol worship.'

'Idol worship?' Hugh repeated, surprised. 'What kind of idol?'

'Specifically, a miraculous head called Baphomet. This head is variously described as dark, even blue-skinned, and bearded. Some say turbaned, some not, but all agree on one point – this thing was alive.'

'Alive!' Hugh's eyes widened.

'Oh, yes. It could speak and see, although it was death to look on it directly. It seems to have been a very dangerous object indeed. There are tales of it being transported from the Middle East in a specially prepared lead-lined wooden casket, a reliquary, such as would be used to take the remains of a saint. The reliquary was guarded at all times by four Knights with drawn swords, standing at the cardinal points of the compass. Despite these precautions, the head seemed to have caused death and destruction wherever it went, on sea or land. There are stories of the uninitiated and over-curious being struck stone dead; of mysterious plagues breaking out in Cyprus, Malta, Marseilles – all the places where the thing rested. Even the sea opened up as it passed, the waters beginning to rotate to create a vast whirlpool. Following vessels were sucked down into this vortex.'

Sally frowned. 'You mean it destroyed friend and foe alike? What's the point of having something capable of doing that?'

'Destruction was not an end in itself,' her father replied. 'It was merely a symptom of the power the head contained. The head had other attributes: it could make the trees flower, the land germinate, and was the source of all the Templars' power and riches. But such power would have to be carefully controlled.'

'How?'

'By ritual magic. Spells cast to contain the force – acting much like the carbon rods in a nuclear reactor. This was probably the nature of the secret heretical ceremonies described by the Inquisition.'

'What were a bunch of Christian knights doing with a thing like that?' Hugh chipped in.

'They probably stole it. The cult of Baphomet must have started in the Middle East and then spread to Europe. There were whispers, rumours, of Templar connections with certain exotic cults which had existed there for hundreds, if not thousands, of years. Of lost valleys and ancient caves, hidden deep in the deserts, which contained secret shrines dedicated, not to God, but to His opposite – the Spiritus Mundi, the Lord of the World. Lucifer, in other words. The Son of the Morning.'

'Lucifer is a name for the Devil, right?' Hugh questioned.

His father nodded.

'Did anyone ever find this head thing, after they were all arrested?'

'No. No one ever did. It was probably kept in their Paris

preceptory – kind of like their European HQ – and everything was taken out of there a couple of days before the arrests. Many believe it survived, many have searched for it over the centuries, but nobody has ever found it.'

'And Templar Knights lived here?'

'Yes, a little group of them. The settlements they established can be identified by the prefix "Temple".'

'What happened to them?' Hugh inquired.

'They were all arrested and imprisoned,' his father replied. 'All except one. There were six Knights here, but only five were arrested. The sixth must have escaped, but there is no record of him. All we have is a name. Stephen de Banville.'

'What about the ones who didn't escape?'

'They were tried, just like their brothers in France, but the persecution in England was rather half-hearted. Nothing as dramatic as that,' he nodded towards the picture of Jacques de Molay, 'ever occurred here. The Order was disbanded and individual Knights were sent off to join other Orders.'

'And that was the end of them?'

'Yes, in a way, but there is still an abiding fascination in anything associated with the Templars. The trouble is, not a lot of it is based on historical fact.'

'And you think this place,' Sally looked around, 'this inn, was their home?'

'Part of it,' her father corrected, 'but it has changed a bit since their day. A good chunk of it is missing, particularly the chapterhouse, their meeting place. It may be underground. That's one of the reasons I want to excavate.'

'Excavate?' Hugh didn't know about this. 'You mean, properly – with diggers and archaeologists? When?'

'Not yet. I'm still trying to set it up.' Philip ran his hands through his hair. 'The complications you wouldn't believe. I had a whole series of meetings organized for the beginning of next week. It took me months to arrange, but try explaining that to your mother.'

'You don't need to cancel them,' Sally said, 'just because we're here. We'll be fine, won't we, Hugh?'

Hugh nodded. They could both see how important this was and Hugh liked the idea of archaeologists. The sooner Dad fixed it up, the sooner the dig could get started.

'I'll go ahead, then. Mrs Harding and Jack will be around. They'll make sure you're all right. I want to get going as soon as possible, sort the facts from local traditions and stories.'

'Stories?' Hugh looked up. 'What kind of stories?'

'Oh, local legends—'

'Any ghost stories?'

'Well, yes—'

'Really? About this place?'

'Yes, as a matter of fact. Plenty. But Hugh—'

'Like what?'

'Don't ask me.' His father shrugged dismissively. 'You know what I think about ghosts and the supernatural. Ask the locals, they'll be keen enough to tell you. It's all nonsense, I don't have time for it. I've got plenty of books on the Templars, though, if you want to know more about them. Would you like to borrow some?'

'Yes,' Hugh replied absently. 'Thanks, Dad.'

All that stuff about the Templars was interesting enough, but ghosts as well! This could shape up into a really decent holiday.

4

Hugh was not the only one who was glad they had come. After she had unpacked, Sally found Will Harding waiting downstairs for her.

'I was wondering,' he pushed a hand through untidy dark hair, 'I was wondering if, er, you'd like me to show you round the village?'

She looked up at him uncertainly, not sure if she wanted company. The day had not been easy, what with the journey and settling into a new place, not to mention the underlying web of family tension. She felt the need to acclimatize, to spend time by herself. Talking to strangers could be hard work, but it looked like he'd made a special effort. He had changed from his working clothes and looked very clean in check shirt and blue jeans. She didn't want to seem un-friendly and, with his brown eyes and tanned skin, he wasn't bad-looking now he'd lost his plaster skim.

'Yes, OK,' she said, and smiled.

He smiled back and accompanied her out through the door.

'Where would you like to start?' he asked, as they left the pub forecourt.

'The church. I've been talking to Dad, about the Knights Templar. He suggested a visit.'

'We'd better hurry up, then. They'll be locking it soon.'

'Locking the church? I thought they were always kept open.'

'Not these days. Just recently there's been an outbreak of vandalism. Might even be locked now. I know where to get the key, though.'

They were walking next to a thick stone wall, low but massively built, which skirted the space between the church and the pub. Temple Field was common land. Scrubby, hummocky, much poorer quality than the surrounding lush green fields, dotted with black-and-white cows motionless as toys on a painted backdrop. A crew of men were putting up a marquee. Will waved at them and got a couple of wolf whistles and a few comments back, some of them pretty graphic.

'Sorry about that. They are setting up for the fête.'

'Oh? When's that?'

'Tomorrow.'

Will was wondering whether to ask her to go with him, and worrying that it was just a boring local village thing, when she asked, 'Do your family come from here? Are you a native?'

'Ooh, arrh.' He squinted down at her. 'Can't 'ee tell? Wait up, m'dear, while I get on me smock an' me gaiters.'

'I'm sorry,' Sally apologised. 'I didn't mean to sound patronizing.'

'That's OK. It's what we yokels expect from you

townies.' He laughed, and some of the awkwardness between them began to melt away. 'Yes, I do come from here. Your brother's been on at me all afternoon, pestering the life out of me.'

'What about?'

Will shrugged. 'Oh, you know, local stories and that.'

'Ghost stories?' Sally frowned. She knew her brother.

'Yes, as a matter of fact. Is that a problem?'

'No, not really. Not unless he tells Bethan.'

'I didn't think of that. Sorry.'

'It's just that she's a bit highly strung, and upset about being away from Mum. I don't want him frightening the wits out of her as well. But it'll probably be OK. Don't worry about it.'

They were approaching the graveyard now. He went to hold the lichgate open for her, but had to stand back. A squat powerful man with a close-cut beard and long dark hair pushed right past them.

'Charming!' Will said, loud enough for him to hear, but he did not acknowledge them. He just walked on, staring straight ahead, as if they were beneath his notice.

Another man followed, about the same age, but balding, with what was left of his hair tied into a ponytail. 'Sorry. After you,' he said and stepped back, smiling an apology.

'Who are they?' Sally asked, after they were through the gate. 'Are they local?'

Will shook his head. 'They are renting a cottage down by Gran's. I don't know what they're doing here. On holiday, I guess, but Gran thinks there is something dodgy about them. Especially the dark one – Holt, I think his name is. The other one seems OK, he comes down to the pub for a drink and a chat, but Holt seems to keep himself to himself.'

'Why doesn't your gran like them?'

'Dunno,' Will shrugged. 'Took against them for some reason, but she's like that. It's best to take no notice. Now, what do you want? Quick scout round or the grand tour?'

He pushed the church door. It was open.

The church was made out of the local red sandstone, with a short tower instead of a steeple. It was dark inside, and cool. It was smaller than she thought, and rather sparse. No pillars, no aisles, just a simple rectangle. Sally stood inside the West Door, looking round. Something about its simplicity, its proportions, its lack of ornament, made it pleasing. Light, striking low through stained glass, spangled the floor with jewelled colours.

Sally leafed through the visitors' book next to the little pile of parish magazines. There were comments from all over the world. Why would people from as far away as America, Canada, Australia, New Zealand and South Africa come to a little place like Temple Marton?

'It's because of the Templars,' Will said, reading her thoughts as well as the visitors' book. 'They come from all over.'

'Why?'

'Because they are fascinated by them.' He looked down at her. 'Aren't you?'

Sally nodded. She felt it, too. The desire to know more about these knights and the mystery surrounding them. Were they innocent, or did they deserve their dreadful fate? Were the accusations of sorcery and devil worship true? What was the dark and terrible secret at the heart of the Order?

'Of course,' Will added, 'most of them are destined to go away disappointed.'

'Oh, why's that?'

'There's not much left from their time here. When the Order was suppressed, the Knights of St John, the Hospitallers, took over until the dissolution of the monasteries, in Henry VIII's reign. After that the church fell into disrepair. What you see here is eighteenth- or nineteenth-century. There's little evidence of original Templars occupation except the rectangular shape, without aisles, and the nine windows corresponding to the original number of Knights in the Order. That's all, so visitors seeking the Templars go away empty-handed – unless they know where to look.'

'Which you do, of course!'

'Of course. Follow me.'

'How do you know so much?' she asked, as they walked up the church.

'It's what I want to do. I'm not a career brickie, you

know. Dad only gave me the job because I need the money and he took pity on me. I hope to be an architect. Now, up here . . . Oh . . .'

'What's the matter?'

He stopped so abruptly Sally nearly fell over him. A rope barred their way. It stretched from one side of the church to the other. A notice, hanging in the middle, said:

CAUTION

DO NOT CROSS THE BARRIER

TO PROTECT FROM THEFT AND

VANDALISM, THIS AREA IS ALARMED

The whole part in front of the altar was cordoned off.

Will leaned over. 'Vicar doesn't hang about. He means business.'

Sally took a step backwards as a wailing sound, thin and intermittent like a burglar alarm, started up.

'Don't worry.' Will looked along the rope. 'I don't think it's wired to anything. I shouldn't think it's going to bring the local constabulary rushing in. Still, it's a nuisance. There was something I wanted you to see.'

'Why do you think they put it there?' Sally inquired, surveying the altar. 'There's not much to steal.'

Will studied the notice. 'It'll be more to do with the vandalism. Like I said, there have been a couple of incidents. Gran's on the flower rota. She says the vicar reckons someone has been in here tampering.'

'What was it that you wanted to show me?'

'Oh, in the crypt.' He gestured towards a little door set into the wall. 'There's some carving. Never mind, maybe another time. There is something over here.'

He dragged a chair to one of the windows.

'Hop up. Look on the sill. Can you see it?' Will brought another chair and climbed up beside her. 'There.'

He was pointing over her shoulder, but she still failed to see. 'Oh, yes. I do now.'

Under his tracing finger, it became clearer. A long straight sword, faintly incised.

'What does it mean?'

'It's a Templar gravestone. According to the practice of the Order, Templar graves were always anonymous. When a Knight died, his sword was laid out on the stone, its outline traced and then chiselled. The carving reflected the exact dimensions, shape and style of his own weapon. He lived by his sword, and that sword marked his place of burial. Neat, isn't it?'

'What's it doing up here?'

'Must have been taken from the graveyard to repair the sill of this window. In the restorations, stone was taken from one place to be used in another. Hang on a minute . . .'

'What is it?'

'Looks like cobblers' wax.' Will scraped at a black line, like a crayon mark, on the edge of the stone and then examined his fingernail. 'You know, like people use for brass-rubbings. And look.' He pointed to a scrap of paper fixed by Sellotape. 'A corner. Here's another. Someone's been taking a rubbing. Another weirdo after Templar memorabilia. Come on.' He helped her down. 'There's another Templar stone outside.'

The grave slab was set low into the church wall. The sword shape looked like an elongated cross, but there was no name, nothing to indicate who it was meant to commemorate, when he died – or how old he was. Sally pulled at the grass growing up over it. There was something else sunk into the soil.

'What do you think this is?' Brushing away loose earth, she showed the object to Will.

'Let's have a look.'

She turned the thin piece of slate over in her hands, offering it for his inspection. It was smallish, oblong, about as long as a postcard but not as wide. One side was plain, the other was covered with symbols. Some were painted, others scratched and incised. Some were vaguely familiar as sun, moon and zodiac signs, but others were strange, written in some secret script. Sally shivered. She had never seen anything like it before, but she felt the purpose behind the circles and crosses and curving lines, and knew it to be sinister.

'That's curious.' Will frowned.

'What is?'

'Second time I've seen one of these this afternoon. Hugh had one. It looked just like it.'

'Hugh?'

'Yeah, he found it tucked against the wall of the pub. Funny how things come in twos.' He traced the carved lines with his thumb. 'It doesn't look old or anything. Show it to your Dad.' He handed the slip of stone back. 'He might know what it signifies. All those signs and symbols have to mean something.'

5

'Ectowhat?' Bethan stumbled over the unfamiliar word. 'Ectoplasm,' Hugh repeated slowly. 'It's psychic snot. It comes out of ghosts' noses. It poured all down here, all down the banisters.' Bethan pulled her hand away, as if the rail was red-hot. 'It took ages and ages to scrub it off. I bet you can still find it, if you look really close. Here's a bit. Do you want to feel? It's all nubbly and crusty. Give me your hand—'

'NO! NO!' Bethan screamed, backing away. Her shrieks brought Sally running up the stairs.

'What's happening?'

'Nothing,' Hugh replied, shrugging his shoulders.

He was trying to look innocent, but Bethan was staring at him. Her look of wide-eyed terror gave Sally a good idea about what had been going on.

'What have you been telling her?'

'Nothing!'

'He has!' Bethan ran to her sister, wrapping her arms around her. 'He's been scaring me!'

'All right. It's all right, I'm here now.' Sally stroked the little girl's springy hair, trying to calm her down. 'Knock it off, Hugh, or I'll tell Dad,' she said to her brother's retreating back. 'You should know better. Why don't you do something useful instead of making up stupid stories.'

'Who said I made it up?' Hugh asked, without bothering to turn round.

'Have you unpacked?'

Hugh went into his room without bothering to reply.

'Why don't you go and do that,' she yelled at the slamming door, 'instead of frightening the life out of Bethan?'

Hugh threw half the contents of his holdall into a couple of drawers, dumped the rest on the floor and then sat down on the bed, unpacking done.

This was a genuine haunted house. Hugh had never even seen one, let alone been in one before. There were stories, loads of them. That kid, Will, had told him all about it when he helped bring the inn sign up here. Hugh glanced over to where the board was propped up against the wall. It looked bigger indoors, and kind of weird. The lurid colours in the turban seemed to shimmer and change, like oil on water, and there was something about the eyes. They appeared to move when he moved, like they were following him . . .

Hugh made himself look away. It was an optical illusion, he told himself, that could happen if you stared at any one thing for long enough. His hand was throbbing again. The bandage had come loose and was all dirty and torn. Maybe Sally would help him re-dress it – that's if she was not still in a stress with him about Bethan. He smiled at the memory of his sister's wide-eyed terror. It had been a good crack, that. He knew he shouldn't wind her up, but what were little sisters for? Will had told him a brilliant story about Bethan's room. The ectoplasm was nothing; he'd made that up. He pictured Bethan, sleeping peacefully. If she only knew . . . Hugh grinned to himself. Sally's problem was she lacked a sense of humour.

'Sally, Sally, wake up.'

Through her dreams she heard her name being repeated over and over again. She muttered a response and turned over, but the voice went on, small but insistent. Finally she opened her eyes to find, as she knew she would, Bethan next to her bed, outlined against the glow of moonlight through the curtains.

'What are you doing here? What's the matter?'

'Can I come in with you?' Her sister was already lifting the edge of the duvet. 'I can't sleep.'

'No!' Sally held the bedclothes down. 'Go back to your own bed.' Bethan had done this all the time straight after Dad left. To let her start again would be to set a bad precedent.

'I can't. I'm missing Mum and there's a funny noise in my room. It keeps going *creak, creak, creak.*'

'Old buildings like this always make odd creaking sounds. It's the timbers settling down. You'll have to get used to it.'

'It's not just the house. It's not just that.'

'Go and see Dad.'

'I did. He told me to come to you. Let me in. Please, Salleee!'

Bethan was wailing now, tugging at the duvet. Thanks, Dad, Sally thought, as she sat up in bed.

'Shh, Beth. Stop that howling or you're not coming in.'

The sobs subsided to hiccups but Bethan continued to plead in an anguished little voice.

'It's a ghost, I know. I can't go back. Don't make me!'

'All right, all right! I'm not sending you back.' Sally moved over to make room for her sister. 'But it can't be a ghost. There's no such thing. Don't be silly.'

'There are! Hugh told me. This place is full of them. They're everywhere.'

'How does *he* know? He's making it up to scare you.'

'No, no! It's true. That other boy, Will, said. I heard them talking when he helped get that horrible picture.'

Bethan stopped, fear cutting her voice to a whimper. She had temporarily forgotten the head thing just down the corridor.

'OK, OK.' Sally pulled the duvet back over both of them. 'You're with me, you're safe. Go to sleep now.'

Bethan burrowed down, thumb in her mouth, and was asleep in seconds.

Sally lay awake for what seemed like hours. Bethan sighed and snuffled and fidgeted. Sally found herself closer and closer to the edge of the bed. For someone so small, Bethan could take up a lot of room. This was Hugh's fault.

44

Hugh and Will. It would soon be light; birds were beginning to sing outside. She would have something to say to those two in the morning.

She could not stay in bed with Bethan a minute longer. The child was deeply asleep but Sally moved with exaggerated slowness and stealth so as not to disturb her. Safely away, she slipped silently out of her room and down the corridor.

Bethan's room was smaller than hers, at the end of the corridor. It was also next to the bathroom. Sally smiled to herself as she slid into the rumpled bed: that explained it. The bathroom belonged to a different age, so did the plumbing. It was tiled in white and black, and the bath was massive with big brass taps. The toilet had a chain on it; maybe someone pulled it. That's what it was. Ghosts! Only someone Bethan's age – only Bethan – could really believe all that stuff. Sally turned over and settled into sleep, satisfied that she had found a rational explanation.

The sound that woke her had nothing to do with plumbing, ancient or modern. Sally lay frozen, listening. It was just as Bethan had described it, a kind of creaking. It was not the random groaning of old timber. It was rhythmic, timed, like something heavy, suspended, swaying slowly back and forth. It could have been the inn sign, moving in the wind, except there was no wind and the cross-ties were empty. And it was not outside, or in the roof, or somewhere unspecified. It was in the room.

She could see nothing, but the sound continued. Slowly,

carefully, Sally slid out of bed. This was stupid, she told herself, but her heart was hammering in her chest and her body was slick with sweat.

It was in the centre of the room. She would have to pass whatever it was to get to the door. She could hardly stand up, her legs were shaking so much. When she moved, the creaking stopped. Through the sudden silence, she made a dash for the door, just as Bethan must have done; but Bethan was small, small enough to avoid collision with anything suspended from the ceiling. Sally was much taller and, as she crossed, she felt something solid spin away from her and something rough, like coarse textured cloth, brush back against her bare shoulder.

Once she was outside, the creaking started up its slow rhythm, like the pendulum of a clock. Sally leaned against the wall, her breath coming in shallow gasps, readying herself for the rush along the corridor.

She gained the sanctuary of her room and slipped into her own bed next to the still-sleeping Bethan. For once, Sally was glad to have her there. She was shivering but the chill she felt was deeper than physical. Only the presence, the warmth of another human being, could dispel it.

6

Sally forced herself to go back in the morning, to see the room by daylight. She opened the door and stood on the threshold, shocked by the ordinariness of pale pink emulsion, flowered curtains and anonymous furniture.

A voice said, 'Hello,' behind her, and she jumped as a hand came down on her shoulder.

'It's me, Will. Sorry, I didn't mean to startle you.'

'You didn't. I mean, you did, but it's all right.'

Sally turned round, trying not to look as confused as she was beginning to sound. 'I thought there were beams in here,' she said, trying to sound casual, aware it was an odd thing to say. 'You know, in the ceiling.'

'There are. Underneath. This is plasterboard.' If he thought it a strange remark, he didn't show it. Instead, he reached up, shifting one of the ceiling panels to demonstrate. 'False ceiling. Walls, too.'

'Why?'

'Someone's idea of an improvement, I suppose.' Will shrugged. 'Although, why anyone would want to take an old building like this and disguise it as a Novotel is beyond me.'

'Do you think you can help me move this?' Sally went over to the single bed and began stripping the sheets.

'Bethan doesn't like it here. She's going to move to my room.'

'Yeah, sure. No problem. Is this going to be a permanent arrangement?'

'For a while. She arrived last night badly frightened.'

'Oh? What scared her?'

'She heard noises.'

'What kind?'

'Creaking, like a heavy weight on a pendulum.' Sally glanced away from him, up at the ceiling. 'It was probably plumbing, though.' As if on cue, a toilet flushed. 'Probably that.' Sally made a joke of it, but the laugh was brittle.

Will looked at her with raised eyebrows. He had a shrewd idea it was not just Bethan who had heard these mystery sounds. 'She'd have to move out soon, anyway,' he said, taking the mattress off the frame. 'We've got to check the wiring in here. It's shot. All needs replacing.'

'Can you do me another favour?' Sally moved to help him. 'Don't talk to Hugh any more about ghosts and stuff. He'll only tell Bethan. He likes to scare her.'

'Right. Of course. Although Bethan wouldn't be the first to have seen, or heard, something unusual or unaccounted for—'

'Oh? Like what?'

He grinned. 'I thought you said not to talk about ghosts.'

'I meant not so Bethan will find out. You can to me.'

'Other people have been woken up by odd sounds,

48

noises, in this room. One woman swore she saw something.'

'Like what?'

'A man at the end of the bed. An old man dressed in black. He was just standing looking at her. She thought he'd wandered into the wrong room, but in the time it took to put the light on he'd gone. She did think that was a bit odd, but she still thought it was a real person. It was only the next day, when she mentioned it to the landlord at breakfast, and he told her that there was no one like that staying here at the time, that she realized there could have been no such person.'

'And?'

'And – that's it.' He smiled. 'Like you said, it's all nonsense to scare little kids.'

'Umm, yes. I guess.' Sally bit her lip and turned away from him, looking out of the window. On this side, the room overlooked the forecourt. This must have been the place where she saw the face, yesterday, when she first came.

'Are you OK?'

'Yes, fine.' Sally turned back, trying to disguise the impact his story had made.

'I better get on.' Will went back to the bed. 'We're knocking off early today, because of the fête. Do you want to come? With me, that is? I mean, it's not very exciting – just the Flower Show, really, and a few stalls and the odd thing going on in the arena, some of them very odd.' He grinned nervously and began twisting the buttons on the mattress ticking. 'But I expect—'

'Yes, sure,' Sally said, cutting off any more apologies, 'I'd love to.'

'Really? That's good.' His nervy grin widened into a radiant smile. 'That's excellent.' He took up the bed's wooden frame, biceps bulging as he turned it on end. 'Now then, where do you want this putting?'

'Did you get to the church?' her father asked when he came in for coffee later that morning.

'Yes, I did,' Sally replied. 'Will showed me round.'

'Bright young man, that. He wants to be an architect. He's been helping me, programming data, building up a three-dimensional computer model of this place.'

'I know,' Sally said.

'How do you know that?' Hugh demanded.

Hugh was possessive, territorial about everything, and had already appropriated Will as *his* friend. Sally had not forgiven him yet for upsetting Bethan, so she put on her best big sister act as she said, 'He told me yesterday.' Sally smiled, making it good and patronizing. 'We had quite a chat. We also found this.' She reached in her bag and took out the tablet of slate with its curious marks. 'It was in the churchyard.' She turned to Philip. 'We thought you might be able to tell us more about it.'

'Let's see.' Hugh leaned across the table and snatched it out of her hand. 'That's not old,' he sneered. 'I've got one of those. Why should Dad be interested?'

'I never said it was.' Sally snatched it back. 'And it's up to Dad to decide whether he's interested or not,' she added, handing the piece of slate to her father.

'I'm going to get mine!'

'Go on, then. Who's stopping you?'

Hugh stood up, pushing his chair back, furious now. Easily riled at the best of times, he was not very good in the morning and, last night, he had not slept well. He had heard Sally moving about, but it was not just that. Vivid dreams had flooded his sleep and he kept being woken up by something, only to lie in the darkness unable to identify what it was.

'Hey, hey, hey!' Their father put up his hands. 'What's got into you two? Let's calm down.'

'It's him!' 'It's her!' they both said together.

'OK.' Philip Goodman steepled his fingers under his chin. 'Sally first.'

'He's been winding Bethan up,' Sally sighed. 'I asked him not to and he still did, so she was in with me half the night because of him and his stupid ghost stories.'

'Hugh?' Philip Goodman turned to his son.

'OK. So what if I did? It was only a laugh. Just because Sally can't see the funny side. She's really getting on my nerves. All of a sudden she thinks she's Mum. Treating me like a stupid little kid all the time.'

'Only because you act like one!' Sally retorted. 'I mean, look at the state of that bandage.' She tugged at the grey, torn tail of gauze dangling from her brother's hand. 'God, Hugh! It'll get infected!'

'See! She's always nagging at me!'

Hugh snatched his hand away and they glared at each other across the table.

'All right, all right! Don't start again.' Their father looked from one to the other. 'First of all, Hugh – I think Sally's right. Wait!' He stopped his son from interrupting. 'Hear me out. You've got to take responsibility for yourself and that means behaving in a sensible way towards Bethan. These stories you've heard, they are all nonsense, like I told you last night, but someone her age is bound to be suggestible.'

'Plenty of people have seen things, heard things,' Hugh said stubbornly. Sally looked at him sharply. The way he said it made her think maybe he had, too. 'Lots of people believe,' Hugh continued. 'It's not just stories.'

'That's up to them.' Philip folded his arms. 'But that's not at issue here. We are talking about telling a little girl, deliberately trying to scare her. Do you think that's right?'

'No,' Hugh muttered. 'But—'

'But nothing. I know the stories. I've heard them myself. It's all up here,' he tapped his forehead, 'in people's heads.'

'Oh yeah?' Hugh was not convinced. 'How do you know?'

'There are plenty of ways of explaining these things.'

'Like what?'

'Well, lots of people who say they have seen these

phenomena *want* to believe in the paranormal, so they set about finding reasons, some cause or other: violent death, suicide, the presence of some magical, venerated object, the site itself having ritual importance. Or it could be some kind of intense emotional atmosphere.' He grinned. 'Some people think poltergeist activity is set off by the presence of young people, adolescents.'

'That still doesn't explain why things happen here, does it?' Hugh waved a hand around, and Sally nodded.

'OK.' His father sat forward, they were going to be harder to convince than he thought. 'One.' He marked them off on his fingers. 'Suggestion. If you *know* other people have seen things, then you are more likely to, aren't you?'

'But why here?' Sally glanced at her brother. 'That still doesn't answer Hugh's question.'

Philip Goodman sighed, trying to read their faces. He hadn't really thought about the pub's haunted status when he bought it. He hoped this wasn't going to be a problem.

'A place like this has a long history.' He spread his hands in explanation. 'Used by lots of people. You are bound to have a fair few deaths, accidents, murders, suicides. Plenty of fuel for storytelling, not to mention a bar-room auditorium, a ready-made and eager audience. Also, drink causes people to see things, double vision, pink elephants – you name it. Quite frankly,' he sat back, arms folded, 'I'm interested in the history here, not a lot of rubbish about ghosts that ignorant people have made up to go with it.'

'But, Dad—'

'I thought you were going to get your slate?' Philip said.

The discussion was over, it was time to change the subject.

The slips of stone, side by side on the kitchen table, were of a piece, the same size, shape, thickness and weight, cut from the same slab of slate. They were not old, not artefacts in that sense, but they were unusual. Both were covered on one side with strings of glyphs or sigils. Magical signs. Some of them Philip recognised. The sun, and the full moon, the sign for Mercury, the zodiac symbol for Leo, but others were much more obscure. The scratched-in carving was not meant to be decorative, it was workmanlike and exact. These stones had been put there for a purpose. But Philip was not certain why. He could not identify them exactly, but he knew enough to recognise that the symbols belonged to the world of spells, sorcery and magic. He frowned: this was puzzling. There were some weird people involved in this sort of thing, occult practitioners, even black magicians. He hoped nothing here was attracting attention from that kind of person.

'What are they, Dad?' Hugh asked. 'What do you think?'

'I'm not sure. Where did you find them again?'

'By the wall outside,' Hugh said.

'This one was at the side of the church,' Sally added.

'Umm. Clive might know.'

'Who?' Hugh asked.

'Clive Rowlands. Young archaeologist I've been working with. He's more into New Age stuff than I am — sacred sites, ley lines, earth mysteries. These slates probably fit into that kind of category. I'll take them Monday; see what he thinks.' He turned the slates towards the kitchen window to get more light. 'Some of the sigils look vaguely alchemical.'

Hugh frowned. 'What, as in "alchemy"? Like old-time science?'

His father nodded.

'But these are modern! I thought alchemists spent their time trying to change lead to gold, and looking for the elixir of life,' Hugh scoffed. 'No one believes in that sort of stuff any more, surely?'

'Yes, they do,' his father replied, 'and that's a very simplistic point of view, if you don't mind me saying so. There are still alchemists who carry on the Great Work. Newton himself, the father of modern science, was an alchemist. It is all about discovering the secret of life, the nature of matter. Isn't that what all scientists are trying to do?' He traced the lines of magical signs. 'The only difference lies in the method.'

7

The Temple Marton Annual Flower Show and Fête was always held on the Saturday nearest to the 1st of August, and always in Temple Field. This arrangement never varied. The village refused to acknowledge that the Bank Holiday had been transferred to the end of the month. They lived by a far older calendar. 1 August was Lammas Tide, a date marked, time out of mind, as the Summer Harvest Festival.

By early afternoon the site was crowded. Stalls lined the whole perimeter. Tombolas and games, coconut shies and hooplas, stood next to tables piled high with car-boot bric-à-brac. Plant and craft stalls competed for space with fortune-tellers, children's entertainers and hippies selling jewellery.

The bottom of the field was marked off by ropes for the different displays scheduled throughout the afternoon. In front of the arena, two marquees stood side by side. One was the tea tent, the other held the Flower Show.

'We'll start there first,' Will said. 'Get it over with.'

'They seem to be taking it very seriously,' Sally commented as Will paid their raffle-ticket entrance fees and they stepped into yellowy sunlight refracted through canvas.

'Are you kidding? This is the most important event of the year for some of them.' The tent was crowded. He indicated the groups of people standing around, arms folded, as white-shirted judges moved down the rows of tables. 'The rivalry is intense. It ranges from not speaking amid accusations of cheating, to dark talk of sabotage. Feuds have started over less.'

It was hot inside the tent, and humid. The sappy smell of trodden grass mixed with the sweet scent of cut flowers. Elaborate arrangements took up long trestle tables. Roses, each bloom matched and perfect, stood next to banks of early dahlias, some huge with shaggy petals, others small, brightly coloured pompoms hardly bigger than golfballs.

The vegetables were arranged with military precision: beans as straight as rows of pencils; potatoes nestling in beds of peat, each one a perfect oval, like clutches of eggs; shallots matched in size, their tops bound tightly with twists of twine. There were specialist sections: vegetables grown for size, huge engorged marrows, onions as big as footballs. And the exotic: courgettes and bell peppers.

'First time I've ever seen a courgette described as exotic,' Sally said.

Will laughed. 'It is in this village!'

Bethan was entranced by the miniature gardens sent in by the children, captivated by the ingenuity that had gone into creating a Lilliputian world accurate to the last detail: pools made of mirrors, alpine strawberry patches, tiny twisted trees with apple beads, individual florets planted to make flower-beds. Feathery fronds of carrot tops, seedling spring onions, stood in neat rows next to matchstick beanstalks wound round with strands of grass. Bethan gazed at them with something in between envy and admiration, and wanted to know if she could enter next year.

'Of course you can, Bethan,' Sally said, and then added quietly, 'if we're here.'

'I'm going to do one, anyway,' Bethan announced, eyes narrowed. 'I'm going to make a study of it.'

'Will you be – here next year, I mean?' Will asked as they left her working out what to do and drifted on to the tables of home-made produce.

'Oh, I don't know, it depends.' Sally stared down at the plates of cakes and breads, jars of home-made jam and honey.

'On what?'

'Lots of things. Why do you ask?'

Will shrugged. 'No reason. Look,' he pointed at a cake with a red rosette, 'Gran's won the fruit cake again.' He smiled. 'She'll be pleased. Dad'll say "typical", like he does every year.'

'Sally, Sally.' Bethan was tugging at her arm. 'Can I go outside?'

Sounds of a band were filtering through the chatter in the tent. Events in the ring were starting.

'Yes, sure.' Sally held out her hand. 'We'll all go.'

A procession of girls was entering the ring. They were dressed in short skirts and spangly tops and playing kazoos and xylophones. Bethan pulled her sister over to the ringside.

'Can we stay for a bit and watch?'

'Of course.' Sally smiled.

Bethan hung on the rope, thoroughly absorbed.

'How long are you staying for?' Will asked, as they watched the columns weaving in and out of each other.

'A couple of weeks. Until Mum comes back.'

'Oh, right.' Will's eyes stayed on the marchers. 'I just wondered. My mum's over there, on the white elephant stall,' he added, changing the subject. 'Would you like to say hello?'

'Yes, OK.'

'White elephants? Where?' Bethan looked round.

'They aren't real ones,' Sally explained, 'it's a word people use to describe a stall selling bric-à-brac.'

'What's that?'

'Bits and pieces. Junk, really. Do you want to see?'

'No.' Bethan turned back to the rows of girls. That sounded boring. 'I want to stay here.'

'Well, all right. But we'll be just over there,' Sally pointed. 'Don't go wandering off, and don't get lost. Bethan, are you listening?'

'Yeah, yeah.' Her sister swung on the rope. 'Soon as they've finished, I'll come and find you.'

'Are you sure?'

'Of course!' Bethan sighed. 'Don't fuss. You're worse than Mum sometimes. Honestly!'

'She'll be fine.' Will took Sally's arm. 'No harm will come to her here. Don't worry.'

The woman running the stall was tall with long dark hair tied back in a loose plait. She was in her mid-forties, and attractive, with tanned skin and clear strong features. Her large dark eyes were the same shade as her son's. They softened when they saw him approach, and kept their welcoming warmth as she turned to Sally.

'You must be Sally. How do you do?' She held out a slender brown hand. 'I'm Lyn. I've heard a lot about you.'

'Oh, who from? I hope it was good.'

Lyn smiled and glanced at her son. 'Oh, yes. Correct in every aspect. I've just met Hugh. We had quite a chat.'

Sally turned round and saw her brother, ambling through the stalls, munching on something he'd bought. He had some kind of purchase firmly tucked under one arm.

'What's he got?' Sally squinted after him, trying to see through the thickening crowds. 'Looks like a skateboard.'

'I have to confess, I sold him that.'

'What is it?'

'A ouija board. Don't worry,' she added, to soften any doubts the girl might have. 'It is very old and battered, half the letters are missing and it doesn't have the planchette, you know the pointer thing? You can't really use it without that. It's more a curio than anything. I did think twice about selling it to him, but someone else was after it, and Hugh even went home to get the money he wanted it so badly.'

'Even so . . .' Sally frowned, not sure it was the sort of thing Hugh ought to have.

'Did I do wrong?' Lyn's expression changed to concern.

'Well, no. But,' Sally gestured towards her brother, 'he shouldn't be messing with things like that.'

'Let him have it,' Will said. 'What harm can it do? He's not a little kid. Lighten up, Sal. You aren't his mother.'

'OK.' Sally smiled. 'Sorry.'

Lyn went off to the tea tent, leaving her son and Sally looking after the stall.

'The other contender for the ouija board,' she said, when she came back with three beakers of tea, 'was that chap there.'

'Which one?'

'The one taking photos. Balding, ponytail, leather jacket. Is his name Garvin?' She turned to her son. 'He and his friend have taken that holiday let down by Mother's.'

Mark Garvin gave them a wave and turned away. He had photographs of all three children, plus Will, and that was enough for today. His partner, Mr Holt, liked to have images of his subjects and it was Garvin's job to take care of it. Sometimes he wanted objects belonging to them, or something more intimate: hair, nails, skin. That could prove more difficult than snapshots. It all depended on Holt's intention, and so far he had just expressed a wish to keep an eye on them.

Garvin was not sure how Holt used the items he called

for. What he termed 'The Great Work' was carried on in obsessive secrecy. But Garvin had seen the results. Holt was a dangerous man; not one to cross. He could mess up your mind, your life, cause accidents to happen. Garvin himself was always very careful to stay on the right side of him.

Garvin looked around nervously. He had already failed to get the ouija board, and Holt had wanted it badly. Garvin had no idea what for, the thing was knackered, half the letters missing, and all battered. Holt had far better examples in his collection, but he had cut Garvin's protests off with a cold glance from eyes like twin black stones. The reasons he wanted it were sentimental, personal. Garvin gave a cynical smile: Holt was about as sentimental as an alligator.

As well as a large collection of occult paraphernalia and ritual objects, Holt owned an extensive library of rare books on magic, some of them priceless, handwritten on vellum. They held no interest for Garvin; most were in languages he couldn't understand, and some of them were downright spooky. Particularly the grimoire, the book of spells, which was bound in what looked suspiciously like human skin, complete with tattooing.

Holt had inherited the core of this collection, objects and library, from an uncle, who had died when he was just a little child. He'd added to it substantially since then, using the inheritance he had also gained, plus the income from the shop that went with it. He searched dealerships, auction rooms, specialist shops, buying and selling all over

Europe. He was as obsessive in this as in everything else, liable to get seriously upset if things didn't go his way. He had recently got very worked up over two particular volumes which seemed to have disappeared from his possession. He had even suspected Garvin of taking them, but what would *he* want with the diaries of Montegue Webster, some obscure local historian? Holt had probably sold them on himself, by mistake, or simply mislaid them in his vast library. He was always telling Holt it needed cataloguing properly.

Mark Garvin cut across the grass and ducked into the Show tent. He didn't want to go back yet. Holt was in a strange mood, had been all afternoon, and sometimes Holt scared him, he didn't mind admitting it. One glance from those basalt eyes was enough to shrivel your insides. So why work for him? The simple answer was money. Holt paid him, and put work his way. Garvin had a record for a string of less than attractive crimes. Without Holt he would have found it hard to make a living.

'Thanks for looking after the stall,' Will's mother said as she sipped her tea. 'Why don't you help yourself to something? It's mostly trash, but if you fancy anything.'

'There was this . . .'

It was a watercolour sketch of the church. Sally had spotted it while they had been left in charge.

'I thought I'd give it to Dad. He likes things like that.'

'You must have it, then.' Lyn put down her cup and

began to wrap it. 'It is rather nice. How about you? What about this? It's silver. A spot of polish will bring it up really well.'

She was holding up a cross on a thin chain.

'How much?' Sally took out her purse, it looked more valuable than the other stuff.

'A gift. Don't be silly.' She fixed it round the girl's neck. 'What about Bethan? Do you see anything she might like?'

'Oh. Er, I don't know . . .'

Sally froze. What about Bethan? She had forgotten all about her. Sally looked around, searching the area. Bethan was nowhere to be seen; she was missing.

'She's not in the middle. She's nowhere round the ring. I'll pick up Hugh and we'll go round all the stalls. If she doesn't turn up, we'll put an announcement over the Tannoy.'

Sally nodded. 'Yes, OK. I'll check the tents.'

Will ran off, leaving Sally standing by herself. It was a bad idea to think the worst, but how could you not? Already, in her mind's eye, Bethan was speeding off in the boot of someone's car. Tears of fear and guilt sprang to her eyes; she smeared them away. That was not helping. Bethan had done this kind of thing before. Suddenly Sally knew exactly where she was. You had to think like Bethan if you wanted to find her.

Sally found her by the miniature gardens, talking to a man. The one taking photographs; the one called Garvin.

'Where have you been?' Sally grabbed her sister's arm. 'We've been looking for you *everywhere*!'

'Ow! You're hurting!'

Sally made herself slacken her hold. Her grip was tighter than intended, but she was so relieved it was as much as she could do not to give Bethan a really good shaking. 'And another thing,' she hissed, 'how many times have I told you not to talk to strangers?'

'He's not a stranger,' Bethan objected. 'He's telling me about how to make the little gardens.'

The man squatting down next to her stood up. 'Hi, my name's Mark, Mark Garvin.' He smiled, revealing a gap and a gold tooth at the side. 'I didn't mean any harm, I swear. I used to make these as a kid, I was just explaining how you do it.'

'Thank you.' Sally's lips were tight, her tone frosted. 'We've got to go now. Say goodbye, Bethan.'

'Goodbye, Bethan.' The man took the little girl's hand in a solemn formal gesture of parting. Then he turned it over. 'Umm, interesting.'

'What is?'

Sally peered down at her sister's palm. All she could see were little grey worms of grime in all the creases.

'Your sister's hand. Very formed for a child. Thin and long with tapering fingers.' He let them go one by one. 'Very sensitive, even psychic.'

'Is that what you do? Read palms?' Sally captured her sister's hand and held it in her own.

'Among other things.'

He passed his own hand behind Bethan's ear. 'Oh, Bethan. What's this?'

He held up a Ping-Pong ball.

'Oh, my goodness, here's another one.' He did it again, with the same result.

'I don't know . . .' Bethan's voice was hushed, her face wrinkling with wonder.

'And another.'

'Do it again!'

'Not this time.' He blew into his fist and, with a turn of the wrist, the balls were gone. 'But what's this?' He passed a hand in front of Sally, appearing to pluck a pamphlet from the pocket of her shirt.

'Me and my partner, we're doing a workshop. Juggling, face painting, a few basic tricks, just for the kids. Wondered if Bethan here might be interested?'

Bethan burrowed up under Sally's elbow to see the piece of green paper. Juggling clowns, rabbits coming out of top hats, black wands in white-gloved hands, surrounded the words:

Tony and Marco
MAGIC WORKSHOP
Teens to tots
Tricks, juggling and lots, lots more . . .
Temple Marton Village Fête

———

Tonight 7.30 p.m. – Temple Marton Village
Talent Show

'Can I go, Sally? Can I?'

'I don't know. Maybe later.'

'No!' Bethan's face set in determination. 'I want to go now!'

The man smiled, gold tooth flashing. He knew he was on to a winner. 'Come on, Sally. Shame to deprive her.' He looked at his watch. 'We're going to be starting soon and it's all free. Won't cost you a penny.'

'Well . . .' Sally pretended to think. She knew she shouldn't give in, but Bethan's face told her refusal was useless. 'Oh, all right, then.'

Bethan jumped up and down, giving her sister a big hug, before running on ahead out of the tent.

'There – you see. It's so easy to make people happy,' he said, as they walked out together. 'Here we are.'

The magic workshop was some way from the other children's attractions, merry-go-round and bouncy castle. It was some distance from any of the other booths, in fact. The fête marshal had tried to move it, but he had just been ignored. The odd positioning did not seem to have affected business: children thronged the roped-off area in front of the tent, playing with the diabolos, juggling balls and clubs which lay scattered in front of the open flaps.

'That's my partner, Tony Holt.' Garvin indicated a man sitting inside the tent, his overweight frame wedged into a flimsy garden chair. Holt wore shirt sleeves, slacks and leather sandals. He was older than Sally had first thought when she saw him coming out of the churchyard. His beard, shaped and sculpted to cheek and chin, was threaded with white, and his long black hair, combed straight back from a pronounced widow's peak, was silvering at the temples. His large dark eyes swept over Sally and she smiled, but he did not smile back. He did not exactly look like her idea of a children's entertainer.

A chalkboard read: *Workshop – 2.30 p.m.* Bethan had already joined the other kids. Only fifteen minutes to the next show.

'She'll be fine,' Garvin said. 'You can leave her with us. Come and get her in about an hour's time.'

'I'll stay, thanks.'

Sally wanted to go, but there was no chance of that. She had to stay with Bethan, who was trembling with anticipatory excitement. It would take a general anaesthetic to get her away from here now.

'More the merrier. I'm sure you will find it instructive. Something for everyone, that's our motto. If you enjoy this, as I'm sure you will, maybe you'd like to come tonight as well? Bring your dad and your brother.'

'How do you know who I am?'

'Your father has just bought the Saracen's Head. And you're here to visit him.' He showed the gap between his

69

teeth again. 'Don't worry. There's no magic. This is just a very small place.'

'You don't live here?'

'My colleague and I,' he gestured towards the man in the garden chair, 'are renting a cottage. We'd planned on staying at the Saracen's Head, but that was before we knew about the change of ownership.' He stroked his chin. 'It's a very interesting place you've got there. Your dad picked it up for a rock-bottom price, so I understand. He's a lucky chap. Quite a bargain. Now, if you'll excuse me, I have props to prepare.'

'I've checked the booths and the stalls,' Will reported as he jogged up to Sally. 'She's not in the tents . . .'

'I found her.' Sally pointed to where Bethan was sitting cross-legged on the ground in front of an older girl applying face paint. Silver bracelets slid up and down the girl's arm as she worked, and the strap of her black vest slipped to show a butterfly tattoo. She wore a nose stud and her ear was fringed with earrings. She was chatting to Bethan. Her long hair – divided into plaits, each one beaded and wrapped – swung this way and that.

'Oh, right.' Will looked down at Sally's troubled face. 'What's the matter?'

'I don't know. Nothing.' Sally thrust her hands into her pockets. 'I – I just don't like these guys. I wouldn't be here out of choice, that's all.'

'Now, boys and girls, the moment you have all been waiting for . . .' Garvin flashed a smile as he appeared through the tent flap. He placed a box on a stand and the girl with the face paints got up to assist. 'First, a few simple tricks.'

'Hey,' Will leaned down, whispering to Sally. 'You don't hang on to things very long, do you?'

'What do you mean?' Sally asked, but her hand automatically went to her throat.

'You've lost that cross. The one Mum gave you.'

'Oh, no.' Sally's hand groped round her neck. 'It must have dropped off.'

She looked down inside her shirt and then back towards the rest of the field, the trampled grass, the walking feet.

'It could be anywhere.' Will shook his head. 'We'll never find it. Never mind, can't be helped. These things happen. What's this?' Will took the flyer from Sally's pocket and groaned. 'Oh, no. Not the Village Talent Show. It's dire. People doing sketches and terrible singing and awful recitations. You don't want to go, do you?'

'Now, if we could have a bit of hush, please.' Garvin was getting ready to demonstrate three-ball juggling.

'Not particularly,' Sally whispered in answer to Will's question.

Bethan turned round, glaring fiercely. 'Shh, you two! The show's beginning!'

'But,' Sally added, with a wry smile, 'I know someone who will.'

Will and Sally settled themselves behind a row of children, all watching Garvin with rapt attention. Sally had never been interested in the intricacies of juggling or magic tricks and her attention began to wander almost immediately. She found herself looking behind Garvin and his young assistant, into the tent. The flap had been released and draped down, but from where Sally was sitting she could see right in. Holt remained in his chair, perfectly motionless – not blinking or moving a muscle – all through Garvin's demonstration. He just sat, staring straight ahead, or he *appeared* to be, it was hard to tell. Perhaps it was the angle Sally was looking from, but it seemed that his eyes had rolled up into his head, as if he was having some kind of fit.

Holt was not unwell, he had merely altered his state of consciousness. He was lost in a deep and profound meditation, from which nothing would rouse him – not even the noise of the Fête, or his partner's patter, or the children's excited shouting. He was concentrating all his being, searching for something. Eventually, he began to relax and his grim expression softened. Only he could feel it, the movement was so slight, but as he continued the meditation the ground beneath his feet started to vibrate, as though deep under the earth something had been activated.

8

By five o'clock everyone was drifting away from Temple Field. The Fête was over for another year. Edna Harding, Will's grandmother, had come back to the Saracen's Head and was having tea at the kitchen table with Sally and her grandson. The house was quiet; all work had finished at midday. Bethan was in the yard, playing with some kittens she had discovered living in one of the outhouses, Philip was working in his study, and Hugh had still to return from the Fête.

The sudden sound, a succession of little percussions, rapid and hollow, was not loud, but it was surprising, and difficult to account for in an otherwise empty house. Edna's deep-set dark eyes opened wide and her gaze darted towards the door. The noise was coming from the direction of the staircase. There it was again, a sequence of tumbling falls. Will stood up. A series of small solid objects dropping on to a hard surface; a sound at once familiar and forgotten, echoing up from childhood.

Marbles cascaded down the stairs, bouncing from one step to another, skittering across the stone floor at the bottom and skittling into each other.

'Shouldn't play with those things on the stairs,' Will's

gran said, frowning and stepping back. 'Someone could go their length.'

Will trapped the last one with his foot and began to pick them up.

'Hugh,' Sally shouted from the foot of the stairs. 'Hugh, are you up there?' This was bound to be down to him. 'Hugh! Can you hear me?' She raised her voice even further. He hadn't been in earlier; he must have sneaked back since. 'Hugh. I'm not telling you again. Come down immediately!'

'What are you yelling up the stairs for?' a voice said from the front door. 'I'm over here. I've just come back from the Fête.'

Hugh stepped into the house, still carrying his parcel.

'Bethan!'

'I've been out in the yard.' Bethan came in from the back. 'What are you shouting about?'

'Come here. Both of you. Do you know anything about these?'

Will held out his hands, the marbles collected in his cupped palms.

'No.' Bethan shook her head.

The cat make-up marks on her face exaggerated the grimace of distaste as she stepped away. She didn't like these marble things; they were not like any she'd ever seen. As Will rolled them round, it seemed like he was holding a handful of eyes: white shot through with red, turning and blind; plain glass with blue and black inside, winking and sly. The biggest one was all pocked and pitted, full of spiralling colours and swirly marks, like the turban on the head thing Hugh had upstairs. A few were dull, brown and grey, made of clay. She couldn't be sure, but it seemed to her that there were mean little faces pinched into the surface.

'Hugh?' Sally turned to her brother. 'How about you?'

'Yeah.' Hugh scarcely glanced; he'd seen them before. 'One of the workmen gave them to me.'

'When?'

'Yesterday.'

'What did you do with them?'

'Put them up in my room.'

'How did they get here?' Sally indicated the stairs.

'How should I know? I've been at the Fête all afternoon. He found them over there.' Hugh pointed to the back door. 'Where they are re-laying the flags.'

'Oh, my Lord.' Edna Harding suddenly looked fearful, her hand went to her mouth.

'What's the matter, Gran?' Will asked, worried that the Fête might have been too much for her, made her unwell.

'I want them put back,' Edna Harding said to him.

'What for?' Will smiled indulgently. 'They're just marbles. Probably fallen down the cracks from kids playing.'

'Maybe.' Edna didn't seem convinced. 'But they need to be put back.'

'Hey!' Hugh protested. 'Hang on! They're mine!'

'Have you got any more things like that?' Edna turned to him.

'No,' he muttered, putting his hand in his pocket.

'Are you sure?'

Her dark eyes seemed to see right through him. Hugh started to blush.

'Well, only this . . .'

He took out the fossil he had found the day before and showed it to her. The tightly coiled spiralling ribs of the ammonite stood out against the flat polished rock.

'I found it over there, above the door,' Hugh added as Edna examined his find.

The object Hugh held was not just any old fossil. Someone had carved the end to look like a snake's head. Edna recognised what it was immediately. Some called it an adderstone, others a snakestone. It was a powerful charm, believed to possess strong protective magical virtue.

'Put it back!'

'But why?'

Hugh started to argue, but Will's gran interrupted him. 'Because it's not just a curiosity, put there for you to help yourself because it takes your fancy. These things were placed at the threshold to guard the house. The marbles were put at the rear to do the very same thing. They're amulets, talismans, to bring good luck and ward off evil. Removing them does the opposite: leaves the house open, and invites in the bad instead of keeping it out. So put it back.'

She watched as Hugh went sulkily over to the doorway to slot the snakestone back with a turnaround jump-shot.

'I'm going up to my room, if that's all right with everyone.' He glared round, before taking the stairs two at a time.

'Gran!' Will protested. She was going way over the top now. If she kept raving on like this Hugh and Sally were going to think them a right load of peasants. 'Surely you don't believe in all that superstition?'

She did not reply, just held out her hand. Despite his objections, Will gave the marbles to her and watched with a despairing shrug as she lowered herself down to scoop away sand and return them to their hiding-place.

'Hey! What are you doing? I laid that sand myself.' Jack Harding stood just outside the threshold, staring down in disbelief at his mother grovelling about at his feet.

'Hello, Dad.' Will looked embarrassed. 'It's Gran . . .'

'I'm putting these back.'

Jack squatted down to see what she held in her hand. 'They're kids' toys, Ma.'

'They ain't. They're more than that. If you, or any of your lads, find anything similar, you just leave it where it is. It ain't to be disturbed. Are you listening to me, Jack Harding?'

She frowned as she dropped the marbles into the small pit she had made for them. These were not playthings, they had been placed there deliberately and should not have been removed. It was hard to make people understand, especially nowadays, but these things were still important.

Now they'd been moved – the lad had taken them upstairs – how had they come back down? There was a deep puzzle here. Edna shook her head. She had worked at the Saracen's, on and off, for a good many years. There had been a time, once before, when things got moved around, appearing and disappearing, for no apparent reason. Such occurrences were called *apports*. Edna knew that because things had got so bad the landlady had called in a psychic. That time the cause had been traced to a guest who had died – a suicide – and eventually the disturbances had ceased.

Edna Harding stood up slowly. There was no knowing what had sparked this off. All she knew was that these amulets had been placed to protect and must not be disturbed – not under any circumstances.

9

'What do you want that stuff for?' Sally asked.

'None of your business.' Hugh looked up from burrowing about in the cleaning cabinet.

'Well, don't make a mess. I've got to get tea ready.' Sally moved around the kitchen collecting ingredients. 'And I don't want things strewn all over the place. Have you seen the books Dad put out for you?'

'Where?'

'On the table.'

Hugh took the cleaning materials he needed and drifted over to look. 'Cool,' he said as he surveyed the titles. 'I'll have a read of those later.' He put them under his arm. 'What are we eating?'

'Spaghetti.'

Hugh made a face. 'Give me a shout when it's ready.'

'Hi, Sal. Where's Hugh?' Sally turned from the stove to see her father coming in through the back door.

'Upstairs. Did you want him for anything special?'

'I just wanted to check he got the books. What are you cooking?'

'Spaghetti bolognese.'

'Yum. Smells good.' Philip Goodman sniffed appreciatively and sat down at the kitchen table. Despite asking about his son, he actually wanted to talk to Sally.

'Have you heard from your mum?' he asked, trying to make the question sound casual.

'No.' Sally sniffed, and wiped her eyes on her sleeve. Chopping onions always made her cry. 'She's only just got there. I expect she'll phone soon.'

'Where was it again?'

'Sardinia.'

'What's this guy like? The one she's gone with.'

'Roger? He's OK, I guess.'

'But you don't like him?'

'I didn't say that. Anyway, it's got nothing to do with me.'

'What do the others think? Hugh and Bethan.'

Sally shrugged. 'He's not around that often.'

'But do they like him?'

'You'd have to ask them.'

'How long has she been seeing him?'

'A couple of months. He's her boss, kind of. She met him when she got her new job.'

'Is it serious?'

Sally frowned. Her father's eyes remained fixed on the table, but his apparent indifference was obviously a facade. She didn't like being questioned like this. It made her feel uncomfortable.

'I don't know.' She paused. 'I don't think so, if you want to know the truth.'

'Oh?' He looked up. 'What makes you think that?'

'Mum doesn't exactly confide in me. It's just a feeling. But she's got a right to her own life. Like I said, it's got nothing to do with me, not really. Or you either, for that matter.'

She turned back to her cooking and began heating oil in a frying pan.

'I know,' her father replied, sounding really miserable. 'It's just I'm concerned about her. We were married for close on fifteen years, after all.'

Sally did not answer. Onions hissed as she threw them into the hot oil. Her father sat in the chair, arms folded, watching his daughter. She had his blue eyes and fair hair, but the shape of her face, the way she held her head, the way she was cooking now, was just like Janet. His wife was the one who had suggested the separation. It had come upon him almost without warning, like a sudden storm.

'I know it was my fault,' he continued, after a moment or two. 'I know that. I miss her, though, and I miss you and Bethan and Hugh. I miss being a family. I still care – I want us back together. If you get a chance, will you tell her?'

'No.'

Sally stirred the onions, watching them brown, turning them over and over.

'Why not?'

'Because it has to come from you.'

'But do you think there's a chance?'

Sally did not reply.

'You're right, of course. Sorry, I shouldn't have asked.'

Philip ran his hand through his hair. 'Seems like I'm getting everything wrong lately.'

'Why did you buy this place, Dad?' Sally asked. 'I mean, if you were thinking about getting Mum back. It's not exactly her idea of a dream house.'

'It might be. Eventually. Aside from the history, it has huge potential. It could be wonderful. If your mum took time to stick around, if she gave me a chance, she'd see it, too. I know her.'

Sally resisted the temptation to contradict that last statement. Her father sat, arms folded, mouth set in a stubborn line. An expression his son had inherited.

'Eventually, maybe . . .' she said diplomatically.

'Well, if you really want to know why I bought it . . .' He paused, then he said, 'Tell me, Sally, do you believe in coincidence?'

She shrugged. 'Sometimes, I suppose.'

'Well, I do. More and more. A chain of events, leading you from one thing to the next. All you have to do is follow—'

'Like what?'

'Like how I came to this place. I was in the local county town, visiting the archive office. It came to lunch-time, and I was a bit peckish, so I went out and bought a pork pie and a coffee from a stand. It was a nice day, so I thought I'd have wander round. Anyway, I found this bookshop, down one of the back streets. From the outside it looked nothing special, just ordinary second-hand stuff, but it had one of my books in the window.'

He leaned across the table, one finger held up.

'First coincidence. I went in, not because of that, not expecting to find very much, but I went in just the same. Once inside, I could see I would have to revise my judgement. The shop contained some rare stuff, mostly arcane and on the occult side, but worth a careful look. Also, the old guy running the shop recognized me. Immediately. He greeted me by name, almost as if he'd been waiting. Second coincidence.' He counted off another finger. 'See what I mean?'

'Not really.' Sally frowned. 'You aren't exactly unknown, he could have recognised you from the book jacket.'

'OK. Try this, then. We get chatting and he says he's had something just come in which might be of interest. An eighteenth-century journal.'

'Why was it so interesting?'

'Because the author was the reason for my visit to the town. He was an antiquarian of some reputation. I'd just been going through his papers in the library.'

'What was your interest?'

'The author, Montegue Webster, lived in the county. Like I said, he was an antiquary, an early historian-cum-archaeologist. He travelled extensively in the Middle East and North Africa, often disguised as a native. He learnt Arabic and translated Moorish works relating to magic and alchemy. Fascinating guy, very learned, very erudite – into all sorts of things including mysticism and the occult. Very contemporary in a strange kind of way. He wrote a series of diaries, journals, thirteen in all, describing his exploits. I was hoping to take a look, but the library did not have a full set. The last but one is very rare – they didn't actually have a copy there – and the final volume is missing altogether.'

'So?'

'So this. The book I was offered was volume twelve of Webster's diaries! The owner of the bookshop wouldn't take any money, said it was a gift. Well—' He shrugged, palms out. 'I wasn't going to pass it up. I thanked him profusely and left the shop. Once outside, I couldn't resist the temptation to take a peek. And, guess what?'

Sally shook her head, she couldn't possibly.

'The first words I read were "Temple Marton"! Webster had a special interest in the Templars and he was involved in the first church renovation. In the eighteenth century. It was restored twice.'

'I know. Will told me. What was the coincidence, then?' Sally asked before the thread of her father's thought unravelled altogether.

'Ah, yes. Right. The book stopped me in my tracks, in the middle of the street. Now, here comes the coincidence bit. When I looked up, I found myself standing next to an estate agent's window and there was the name again, Temple Marton. I was looking at the details of a pub called the Saracen's Head.' He sat back. 'How about that?'

'Yes.' Sally had to agree that was a coincidence.

'I went in and made an offer on the place there and

then.' Her father sat forward in his chair, hands on the table, face creased in earnestness. 'I feel I was guided here, why I'm not sure yet, but I haven't regretted the decision, not for a minute.'

'What else is in the diary?'

'All kinds of fascinating stuff!' Philip spread his hands wide. 'I haven't had time to verify any of the claims he makes, but that's where I read about the magical head, Baphomet, and its journey from the Middle East. He seems to have seen the head as a living repository of all kinds of ancient and arcane wisdom, maybe all knowledge.'

'Where did all this knowledge come from?'

'From the Arabs, when they invaded what they called the land of Khem. Khem was Egypt, that's where we get the terms "alchemy" and "chemistry". The Arabs learnt from the Greeks, who in turn had learnt from the Egyptians. Just think, thousands of years of uninterrupted knowledge, stretching back to the priest cults of Ancient Egypt. According to Webster, this knowledge was stolen by the Templars and transported to Europe inside the head of this thing called Baphomet, and it was this which gave them all their wealth and power.' Philip Goodman smiled. 'Montegue Webster was most probably completely crazy, but you have to admit, it is an interesting theory.'

Hugh was so absorbed in what he was doing that he forgot everything else. He didn't even hear Sally calling him for tea. Hugh gave the ouija board a last rub and sat back to admire his handiwork. The board had come up nicely, it only had a few letters and numbers missing and that was easily put right with the help of Bethan's paint set.

Using his hand for a guide, he'd drawn a leaf-shaped pointer on an offcut he had acquired from a pile of wood downstairs. The lady at the Fête had called this part the planchette. He had tools for shaping and glue for sticking – all he needed was a set of little wheels for it to run on. A trip to Bethan's toy box would solve that problem.

He jumped at the sudden knock on the door.

'Sally says if you don't come now, she's feeding yours to the cats.' Bethan's voice came through the wood.

'OK, OK. I'm coming.'

He stroked the board one last time for luck. He'd soon have it in working order. The thin plywood, warm from the afternoon sun, shining and honey-coloured, seemed to vibrate at his touch.

10

TEMPLE MARTON —
ANNUAL TALENT SHOW AND GALA

Announced the bunting draped across the front of the village Hall.

WELCOMES ALLCOMERS

'Can anyone have a go?' Sally asked as they went in.

'Oh, yes,' Will said, 'as you'll see. Talent is definitely not a necessity. There's Gran.'

Edna had saved seats next to the aisle about halfway up the long room. Sally sat by her and Will put Bethan on his knee. The place was filling up quickly.

The lights went down and the compère came on to a thundering piano roll. He told a few jokes and introduced the acts. Everyone seemed to know all the jokes and to have seen all the acts, but that did not stop the affectionate applause and genuine laughter. Sally found herself joining in and Bethan loved everything, especially the children singing and dancing.

'We are honoured to have with us tonight two people famed for their magical skill, practised in the art of illusion. Ladies and gentlemen, will you welcome Tony and Marco!'

The pianist banged out the opening chords of *That Old Black Magic* to herald the Tony and Marco Magic Show.

A hush of anticipation spread through the hall: no one had seen these two before, they were an unknown quantity.

They came on to the stage, dressed identically in black trousers and baggy white shirts. Their performance began with a series of fairly unremarkable magic tricks, sleight of hand mostly, executed by Garvin, stage-name Marco. Tony Holt did not really take part in any of this, except to assist, but he showed himself to be an accomplished escapologist. There were *Oohs* and *Aahs* as he methodically extricated himself from a complex arrangement of chains. Stout padlocks, each one tugged and tested by a member of the audience, snapped back at his touch. He sloughed off the heavy iron coils with a shrug and they fell to the floor with a dramatic rattling crash.

He stepped out of the links piled round his feet and bowed his head slightly to acknowledge the rapturous applause. Marco now came forward, appealing to the audience for victims willing to submit to his powers as a hypnotist. Edna looked on, arms tightly folded, face pinched, as the stage became crowded with willing participants.

Edna's disapproval grew as the spectacle unfolded, but the rest of the audience thought it hilarious. Family and friends rocked with laughter, wiping away tears, at the sight of their loved ones lying stiff as boards between two chairs, howling like dogs, grunting like pigs, scratching like chickens.

Mark Garvin grinned at his own success. This part of the show always went down the best.

'I will count back from three, and you will all wake up,' he said eventually. 'Three, two, one!'

He clicked his fingers and, one by one, his victims straightened themselves up and began to look around. Fresh peals of laughter greeted their bewilderment.

'Just a bit of fun, I hope you all agree,' the hypnotist added, clapping each one on the back as they stumbled sheepishly off the stage. 'And now,' he went on, when the last one had gone, 'for our finale. I'd again like to ask for your co-operation. Tony, if you please . . .'

Tony brought a chair centre stage and seated himself. Marco shook out a long silk handkerchief and wound it round his colleague's head several times. He then invited a member of the audience to come up and test the blindfold.

'What are they doing now?' Bethan whispered, transferring herself to Sally's lap. She had followed the rest of it easily enough, but could not puzzle out what was going on at the moment.

'I'm not sure,' Sally whispered back. 'Ssh, a minute and maybe we'll find out.'

'I will pass amongst you with this.' Marco flourished a top hat as he came down the steps. 'Feel free to put in any item you like. Give me your valuables. Stand and deliver!' He grinned again, finger held like a gun to the head of someone in the front row. 'Only kidding, ladies and gentlemen. All items will be returned, naturally. Anything will do, no matter how small, but it must be personal to you. Meanwhile,' he gestured towards the stage, 'my colleague here will use his psychic powers to tell us, not only what the item is, but also something about the owner.'

He passed along the rows collecting things – watches, brooches, rings – before returning to the stage.

'Now, Tony, will you please tell me . . .' he picked out a wedding ring, making sure the audience could see. 'What is this that I am holding?'

Tony sat still on his chair, blindfold eyes staring ahead, face set. The audience went pin-drop quiet, as though they were trying to aid his concentration.

'A ring. Wedding ring. Plain gold.'

Marco mimed amazement and the audience gasped. Marco put his hand up, quelling the scatter of applause. 'I must ask for quiet. That is not all.' He handed the ring to his colleague. 'Now Tony, tell us if you would, to whom does this ring belong?'

'A lady. I see the number four and flowers, I see flowers . . .'

'Would the owner please stand?'

Somewhere near the front a woman stood up.

'Lady in a flowered dress, four rows back. What do you think of that, ladies and gentlemen?'

Applause filled the hall. They thought it was fabulous.

The next item out of the hat was a gold pocket watch. Again, Tony guessed what it was.

'The owner is an older gentleman,' he said, holding the watch between his two hands, 'sitting at the back of the hall. Not very tall, rather stout, if he doesn't mind me saying. The watch doesn't work, hasn't for a long time . . .'

The hall erupted with laughter as a Joe Haines stood up, waistcoat strained to bursting over his ample stomach. 'That's mine.' He looked round. 'And he's right. Ain't worked for thirty years. I only wear it for show.'

Tony returned the watch to Marco, who held it to his ear.

'It does now.' He handed the item back to its owner.

'By damn. It does and all. Right time, too.' Joe Haines stared down at the timepiece with a shake of his head. He looked out at the audience. 'Who'd have thought it?'

The two men had them then. They could have gone on all night, but for the fact that there were other acts to follow.

'Time for one more only, I'm afraid.' Marco rummaged in the hat for a final time to calls of 'Do mine', and groans of disappointment. 'Now Tony, could you tell me for one last time what exactly do I have in my hand? And who owns it?'

91

'What is it? What is it?'

Bethan bounced about on Sally's lap, trying to get a better look.

'I can't see anything, if you do that. Stop wriggling about.' Sally peered round her sister, but the object was so small it was impossible to identify from this far back. Something on a chain. The pendant swung this way and that, but failed to catch the light.

'I see a chain. A cross on a chain,' Tony declaimed. A murmur from those close enough confirmed what he was saying. 'But not a crucifix,' he went on. 'The shape is unusual.'

Marco swung it so the front row could identify his accuracy.

'Right on all points. Now, Tony.' He caught the cross and dropped it into his partner's hand. 'Tell us about the owner.'

Tony held it for a moment, rubbing it between his palms. 'A woman. A girl. Young. This has not been in her possession long. She is pretty. I see blue, her eyes are blue, I think. And yellow. Yes. Her hair is yellow and she is also wearing a yellow shirt, T-shirt, maybe . .?'

Sally turned, like everyone else, to see who he could be talking about.

'She is near the centre aisle, about halfway back.'

Sally looked round again and then realized that everyone was staring at her.

'Anyone here? Anyone?'

Marco had retrieved the cross from his friend and was advancing down the hall. Will took Bethan off Sally's lap. People around were urging her to stand up.

'But I didn't put anything in the hat,' she said to Will, feeling herself colouring up.

'Maybe not,' Will whispered back, 'but it's yours, isn't it? It's the cross you lost. The one Mum gave you.'

'Ah . . .' Marco was next to her now, standing over her. 'I think we've found the young lady in question. This yours, sweetheart?' He held the cross up. It shone now, gleaming and glittering in the light. 'There you are, reunited with your property. Good as new. Better, in fact.' He bent towards her. '*Croix Patte*. Cross of the Templars,' he whispered as he parted her hair to fix the catch, 'but I expect you know that. Tony's put a bit of a shine on it for you. Now,' he added, his voice louder, 'show the ladies and gentlemen.'

He pulled her to her feet and Sally stood awkwardly, silver cross bright against her yellow T-shirt. She turned round slowly, to gasps of wonder, people saying to each other, 'How does he do that?'

'Well, that concludes our show for tonight.'

The rest of his words were lost in thunderous applause which continued until Marco and Tony had left the stage and the compère came on to announce the interval.

The audience made their way towards the refreshment tables at the back of the hall, talking excitedly. Tony and Marco had caused quite a stir. Several people stopped Sally to look at the cross she was wearing and exclaim over the wonder of it.

'What do you think, Gran?' Will handed her a mug of tea.

'Charlatans and mountebanks,' Edna sniffed.

'How do you know, Ma?' Jack Harding laughed.

'Shifty eyes, the pair of them.' Disapproval turned to distaste as she took a sip of her drink. 'This is as weak as dishwater. Who made this tea?'

'Someone's in trouble,' her son remarked as she went bustling off towards the bank of urns on a side table. 'How do they do it?' He turned to his son. 'Seriously, though.'

'Two ways,' Will replied. 'First, they could be signalling to each other.'

'How can they do that?' his mother asked.

'Some kind of code they have developed, contained in the words they use and intonation. For example, the sender might say, "Please could you tell me . . .", which means, "I'm holding a watch", or, "Tell me, please . . .", which means a ring.'

'Oh, right,' his mother replied, 'but how does the other one know who owns it?'

'Same way,' Will explained. 'Different code. Like when he hands it over, he might put three fingers on the other guy's shoulder, which means three rows back. Either that, or there really is some kind of genuine telepathy between them, with the receiver using psychometry to "read" the object.'

'Psychowhat?' Jack Harding's wide brow creased. 'Kid always sounds like he's swallowed a dictionary.' He looked at Sally, who shrugged. She'd never heard the word, either. He turned back to his son. 'You've lost us now.'

'Psychometry is like picking up the vibe. You hold whatever it is in your hand and you pick up stuff about it. Who it belongs to, when they lost it, like that. As though each thing has its own history locked into it. Some people reckon it can be used to find out about artefacts from the past – kind of like psychic archaeology. It's very interesting.'

'Interesting, maybe.' Jack Harding looked down at his feet. 'But I don't buy it. I reckon they were cheating.'

'Signalling, you mean?' Will nodded. 'Yes, probably. But it's part of their act. It's not exactly cheating, Dad.'

'I'm with your gran on this one.' Jack glanced over to where the two magicians were standing surrounded by admirers. 'Pair of tricksters, if you ask me. What do you think, Sally?'

Sally held up the cross round her neck, watching it catch the light. 'I'm not really sure . . .'

The cross had been lost, now it was returned. Good as new. Better in fact. It had gone from her tarnished and come back shining. And how had Garvin acquired it? If he had found it, how had he known it was hers? Had he stolen it away from right under her nose? Sally had no answers. Perhaps it was magic after all.

★ ★ ★

Bethan was too tired for the second half. Will carried the little girl home on his shoulders and Sally put her to bed. When she came downstairs, Will asked if she would like to go for a walk.

'Yeah, sure,' Sally smiled. 'Hugh's in his room. Dad's working. Bethan's sleeping. So it's either that or the telly, and it really is a lovely evening.'

The sun had already set, staining the horizon red, but it was still warm and the sky overhead was blue and luminous. Will led her by the hand and cattle turned to stare incuriously as they walked through fields waist-high with seeding grass and creamy fronds of meadowsweet. They crossed one stile and then another, the path marked by blunt yellow arrows, until they came to the edge of a wood. Here the path widened out to a broad green bridle-way.

'At one time Temple Marton would have been completely surrounded by woodland, stretching for kilometres in every direction.' He held his arms wide. 'The village must have been pretty isolated; still is in some ways. This is like one little bit of that huge forest. Used to be able to hear nightingales on warm summer evenings like this,' he said, as he put his arm round her.

'I'm not surprised.' Sally looked up at the big trees, almost expecting her voice to echo, like in a cathedral. 'Can you still?'

'I don't know.' Will shook his head solemnly. 'I'm not sure what they sound like.'

Sally laughed. 'Neither am I. Still, it's a nice idea. Which way now?'

They had reached a fork in the green road.

'This one, I think.' Will ducked under a low branch. 'We'll take the one that's less travelled. Look.'

He was leading her along, walking in front. Suddenly, the path opened out. Sally saw a thick bed of reeds, heard the sharp *chuck, chuck* of a moorhen and ducks' cackling chatter. A flat expanse of water spread in front of her, mirror-still. A swan came from under overhanging trees in a surging glide, arrowing the blue, so the first faint reflected stars were lost in the rippling surface.

'What a magical place!'

'I thought you'd like it.' Will smiled.

'It's beautiful. I love it!'

Will looked at her, his smile softening, growing more tentative, as his arms went round her. 'So are you,' he said, and kissed her.

'Don't get me wrong,' he added, after a moment or two, 'that's not why I brought you here.'

'Isn't it?'

She laughed up at him, her hair pale in the fading light, her eyes as blue as the lake they were standing beside.

'This is the Mere.' He looked away from her, out across the expanse of darkening water. 'It's the other half of Temple Marton, where the place gets its name from.'

Sally shook her head. 'I don't understand.'

'Mere-ton, Maer-ton, Marton.' Will laughed at her

puzzlement. 'You have to say it with a local accent. At one time the Mere would have stretched to the river. It must have been possible to get up here by boat.'

They walked on until they came to a tiny beach. Will looked out at the full moon rising over the sheet of water.

'It's an image I carry in my head,' he said after a moment's silence. 'For me, this is the lake of memory, of imagination. In school when we read poetry, *Morte d'Arthur*, *The Lake Isle of Inesfree*, *La Belle Dame Sans Merci*, this is the lake I see.'

It was so quiet, the silence only broken by small sounds, a fish rising, swifts and swallows shrilling as they looped and turned, flying intricate patterns, swooping low enough to threaten the glassy surface, soaring up to be lost – black specks against an ever-darkening blue.

'It's a really beautiful evening,' Sally said. 'It's still so warm.'

'There's a chance on the way.' Will looked up. 'There's going to be a storm.'

'How can you say that? There's not a cloud, the sky was red—'

'I can tell.'

'How?'

'Runs in the family. Grandad Lawrence, my mum's dad, was famous for it. Farmers would consult him to find out when was best to sow seeds, or reap, or whatever. Locals swore he was a lot more accurate than the TV weather presenters. Maybe not tomorrow, or the next day, but there's going to be a storm. Take my word.'

Sally looked at him, half laughing, wondering whether to take him seriously. 'How do you know?'

'There.' He pointed down at her at her pale primrose T-shirt. 'Can you see them? Little black insects. They are on me as well. The locals call them thunder bugs. There were none out yesterday, and now look. There will be more tomorrow.'

'Ugh!'

Normally insects did not faze her, but that did not mean Sally liked them crawling all over her. She put her hand up to knock them off.

'They're in your hair, too.' Will combed his fingers through, twining the strands round his hands, pulling her to him. 'They seem to like yellow.'

It was almost dark before they thought about returning. Holding hands, they crossed Temple Field approaching the Saracen's Head from the back.

'Who owns this field?'

'No one,' he answered, surprised. 'It's common land. Why do you ask?'

'Just wondering. I thought, if it belonged to Dad, or you could hire it out, you could put a pony on it. There are stables at the pub.'

'Do you ride?'

'Used to. And it'd be nice for Bethan.'

'I don't know if it'd be a good idea. For one thing Gran

99

says beasts don't prosper on Temple Field, and for another, it's like the village green. Used for the Fête and Bonfire Night, things like that. But there's plenty of other land round here.' He paused, not daring to ask her, then he said, 'Does that mean you are thinking of staying?'

Sally smiled. 'It's just an idea. I like it here.'

'What about the others? What about your mother? Would she like it?'

'Not as it is now. She'd hate the mess, but I think she'd like it once all the work was done. She's thinking of going freelance, so she could work from home.'

'What does she do?'

'She's an artist, a graphic designer.'

'Dad could convert one of the outhouses, and make it into a studio for her.'

Sally nodded. It would be nice. More than that. It would be wonderful to heal the fracture in their lives. There was enough space here for everyone to do what they wanted. Might it be possible? Sally shook her head. She had to stop herself. What was she doing? She could not allow herself to be seduced into thinking about it.

'I'd like it,' Will said quietly. 'If you stayed, I mean.'

'Would you?'

'Of course. I already can't bear to think of you leaving.'

'We've only known each other a day.'

He stroked her face, his own looming white towards her.

'Sometimes a day is all it takes,' he murmured and kissed

100

her again, longer this time, deeper and more searching.

Sally fell back against the wall behind her, Will's hands either side of her head.

Suddenly he broke away from her. 'That's funny . . .'

Sally opened her eyes, surfacing as if from a dream. 'What is?'

'This wall.' He touched it again, testing with his fingers.

'What about it?' Sally put a hand against the plaster.

'Can't you feel it? It's as if the whole thing's vibrating.' He moved his hands down and sideways. 'It's stronger towards the base. Like there's a generator in the cellar. But the pub is on the electric mains. That's very strange.'

He held a little slip of stone in his hand, like the others they had found. It was clean, no earth was clinging to it. It was as if it had been freshly placed.

'Where did you find it?'

'Down there.' He knelt down, replacing the sliver of slate in a small cavity at the base of the wall; put it in, and the vibrations started up again; take it out, and they stopped. It was almost as if the thing acted like some kind of key.

11

Hugh heard Sally come in and go to bed. The landing light went off, but his stayed on. He didn't read that much as a rule, but the books his father had lent him were interesting. In his estimation, these Templar Knights – in fact the whole Order – were pretty cool. They took anyone, no matter what they might have done, murderers, thieves, you name it. Knights were going to die anyway, fighting for Christ, so all sins were forgiven. Templars lived like monks, but they fought and died like professional soldiers. Totally dedicated fighting machines, in battle they neither gave or accepted any mercy. If they were captured, they were usually executed straight away because they were such fierce warriors.

The names of the places echoed through Hugh's mind. Ascelon; Acre, with its Accursed Tower; Jerusalem, the Temple of Solomon. Pictures flashed in his head: terrible sieges with blood running in the streets, fierce battles under the gruelling sun, knights charging on huge warhorses, swords wheeling, armour glittering, black-and-white banners flying, an awesome sight, frightening enough to turn the blackest hair white.

After the battle, the Knights would return to their specially built garrisons, castles built in impossible places, perched like falcons' nests, high on impregnable crags and cliffs. Castles with romantic names – Castel Pelerin, Castel Rouge, Belvoir.

Hugh read on, eyes scanning the page. Their story was as exciting as any novel. When the Knights were forced to leave the Middle East, the odds against them just too great, Hugh felt sorry. The Holy Land was home to them, Europe was foreign. Life in the Holy Land sounded much more interesting than what they were going to find at home. They were closer to the enemy they left behind than the ones they were going to join. For them, 'Paradise lies under the shadow of swords', just as it had for Saladin.

Hugh wondered what they did when they came 'home': retreat into themselves, into the Order with its secret rituals and complex inner life. Their meetings sounded like King Arthur and his Round Table. All the Knights gathered in the chapterhouse, sitting in a circle. Two Brethren stood guard, swords drawn. To betray the Order in any way, to reveal its secrets, to disobey, meant expulsion – or worse. They had their own prisons. Knights were walled up and left to die for disobedience.

They were a law unto themselves, governed by their own Rule, only accepting discipline from their own superiors. No one else. That was one of the reasons they were persecuted.

The accusations made against them were what you'd expect to be thrown at any group of heretics. But one indictment was different: no other sect was accused of anything like it. This was what made them special.

The miraculous head. Baphomet. In French *maufe*, 'demon thing'. Eye-witness testimony told of the Templars worshipping the embalmed head of a man, dark-skinned, bearded, with 'hollow, carbuncled eyes, glowing like the light of the sky'. The head was alive. It could speak. One of the accounts hinted at horrible sacrifices made to placate this terrible object of worship. The night was warm, but Hugh shivered as he read on, imagining a stone room, lit by flickering torches, the Knights prostrate in front of their idol. Anyone who saw it happening – anyone unauthorised – simply disappeared.

Hugh wondered about the Knights who lived here, in this house. Did they do anything like that? Was there some secret chamber here – some hidden crypt where all kinds of unspeakable rituals took place? The thought of that was like icy water trickling down his back. He put the book down and drew the duvet up to his chin, but still he could not stop shaking. Was it his imagination, or was the room getting colder? Hugh's breath steamed in front of his face. He blinked in disbelief. The temperature was plummeting. He shook his head. This could not be happening. Hugh swung his legs out of bed, the floor was freezing cold to his feet. He could not go to Sally or Dad. They would think he was as bad as Bethan. He'd go downstairs and get a drink. When he returned, the room would be normal.

★ ★ ★

A noise from outside the bedroom jarred Sally from her sleep. Something falling, glass smashing. She lay in the dark, listening intently, wondering if it had been real or in a dream, and if anyone else had heard it. There was no following sound behind her sister's slow, regular breathing. Maybe she was the only one awake. Maybe someone had broken in. Maybe there were burglars. She would never get back to sleep again if she did not go and investigate.

Hugh was standing on the landing, facing away from her, looking down at the banister.

'Hugh?'

He jumped at the sound of her voice. 'Watch out. I dropped a glass.'

His voice was thin and shaky, his face as white as the milk pooling and dripping down the stairs. Sally picked her way through the scattered shards.

'Hugh? What's the matter?' Sally put her arm round him. He did not shrug her off as she half expected. He was scared, very scared. She had not seen him as frightened as this, not since he was a very small child.

'I – I, I don't know. I—'

'What were you doing? Start at the beginning. Take your time.'

He glanced back down the stairs.

'I – I couldn't sleep. I went downstairs to get milk. On the way back . . .' The words tailed off. He had to recall himself. 'On the way back, I thought I saw something. It gave me a shock.'

'What was it? What did you think you saw?'

'A white shape, but it was, like, there,' he held both hands out, 'and moving through things. It went towards the wall and, as I watched, it went down and down, like that,' he said, demonstrating, going lower and lower, 'down into the floor.' He paused for a moment. 'But that's not the worst thing—'

Sally held him tighter. He was quivering under the skin like a dog.

'What is it, Hugh?' she whispered. 'Tell me.'

'It was, it was this . . .'

He gingerly touched the banister and then withdrew his fingers and began wiping them on his pyjama top.

'What?'

Sally peered down but could see nothing unusual. The banister looked as it always did, its polished surface shining faintly in the filtered moonlight.

'I put my hand out, to steady myself, and it was like I got stuck to it. Like the banister was covered in some horrible gluey stuff.' He shivered. 'It was disgusting, all cold and icky and gooey.'

He wiped his hand again and again.

'There's nothing there now.' Sally touched the wood. It felt perfectly smooth and satiny.

'But it was there, Sal. It was ectoplasm, like I told Bethan. And there was another thing, a vibration, like the whole thing was shaking. I couldn't take my hand away. It wouldn't let me go.'

'I'd better get Dad.'

'No, don't.' Hugh clutched her arm, pleading. 'He doesn't believe in things like that. He'll think I imagined it – or made it up. Promise you won't tell him.'

'OK.' Sally agreed, reluctantly. 'Let's get you back to your room. Try and forget about it. Try and go to sleep. Things will look better in the morning.'

Hugh could not sleep. The temperature in the room seemed normal, but he shivered, cold and hot at the same time, like when he had chickenpox. He tried lying still, eyes closed, but his mind was going at a million kilometres an hour, racing through a maze of full-blown imaginings, technicolour fantasies. Then, one by one, these thoughts started to disappear. They began to focus down to one thing, a feeling that there was someone, or something, in the room with him. Something pulsing waves of malevolence and hate towards him.

The sensation was strong enough to cause the short hairs on his neck to stir and rise like hackles. His breath came shallow and audible, sweat trickled in tiny streams, down his chest and under his arms. He had to turn. He had to see what it was.

The thin curtains failed to keep out the summer night. The room was bathed in the bluish metallic light of a full moon. Over in the corner, the flat surface of the inn sign seemed different. Shadows were thickening round it, blotting out the background. The head itself appeared solid and transparent at the same time, like a hologram. It had gathered dimensions and, all of a sudden, the eyes seemed alive, the shiny black pupils expanding, adjusting to focus. The eyes gleamed, watching him, moving of their own accord as Hugh turned his own head slowly from side to side.

Turning on the light made no difference. The low-wattage bulb only created more shadows. Hugh got up and threw his shirt over the painted face, but he could still feel the eyes through the fabric. Bethan was right – he should never have brought it in – but he could not take it out now. He didn't dare venture out of the room again. He was caught between out there and this thing.

There was only one option. He grabbed the sign and dragged it to the wardrobe. Coat hangers swayed and tinged as he heaved it inside and locked the door.

He felt a lot better then. Reading about that head thing, that Baphomet – that was probably what caused it.

He drifted off to sleep, fingers curled around the wardrobe key under his pillow, but his dreams were uneasy. Something unspecified was pursuing him. It was blind now, but still it came, hunting by smell, snuffling and sniffing, scenting for him. It was near, coming nearer, he could hear its sibilant liquid whispering . . . Hugh jerked awake, terrified, desperate to leave the dream behind, but the sound did not stop. It was here in the room with him. He swallowed back a scream; it was coming from the wardrobe.

Hugh was not a coward. Fight fire with fire, that was his usual way of dealing with things. He would do something about this, he wouldn't let it beat him, but not now. All he could do for the moment was put the pillow over his head and pray for morning to come.

12

Hugh got up at first light to clean the milk and glass from the landing and top of the stairs. Then he dealt with the inn sign, manhandling it on his own and taking it down the corridor to Bethan's old room.

The room had been cleared ready for work, the carpet rolled up and the furniture covered. Hugh took a dustsheet and wrapped it round and round the sign, reducing it to a shapeless bundle. Then he turned it to face the wall and jammed it behind a chest of drawers. He locked the door and left, dusting his hands. He told himself that if the thing bothered him again, he would burn it.

He was eating his second breakfast by the time Bethan came into the kitchen. 'What's the matter with you?' he asked through a mouthful of cereal.

'I couldn't sleep.' The little girl yawned and rubbed her eyes. 'Sally was making noises all night.'

'What kind of noises?' Hugh put down his spoon.

'Sniffling and snuffling noises, like this.' Bethan sniffed to demonstrate, tilting her head and lifting her upper lip. 'And a funny sort of whispering. I didn't like it. It wasn't very nice. What you eating?'

'Cornflakes.'

'Can I have some?'

'Just finished the packet.' Hugh wiped his mouth.

'What's left?'

'Rice Krispies.'

'I don't like those.' Bethan pulled a face. 'I don't like the crickling.'

'That's all there is.' Hugh grinned. 'See you, Bethan.'

Bethan's mood was not improved by Sally pouring her a big helping and then saying if she didn't eat it, she couldn't go out to play. Will came in to find her sitting at the kitchen table, sullen-mouthed and tearful, a bowl of cereal turning to mush in front of her.

'What's the matter with *her*?' he asked.

Sally glanced at her sister and turned her eyes to the ceiling. 'Don't ask. She won't eat and she's mad at me for some reason. Bethan — eat your breakfast!'

The bowl careered across the table, the spoon depositing soggy Rice Krispies and milk on the scrubbed pine surface. Bethan hid her face behind a pair of grubby fists, her hair standing out in hopeless tangles.

'She won't do anything. She won't let me brush her hair, or wash it.' Sally shook her head. 'Everything is going slightly pear-shaped, to be honest.'

'Don't talk about me like I'm not here!' Bethan shouted, taking her hands away from her face. 'I'm not eating that stuff — it's scum!' She stared at Sally, eyes narrowed, finger pointing. 'You pull, and you use stingy shampoo. Not like Mum!'

'She didn't sleep very well last night,' Sally said,

searching for an excuse for her sister's behaviour. 'And one of her favourite cars is missing. She's got hundreds. How she knows one's gone is a mystery.'

'I know, because I count them. And I haven't got hundreds, I've got forty-three.' Bethan studied her bitten nails. 'It's the one Dad gave me. The ghost took it.' It looked like she was about to start crying. 'It belonged to Barbie.'

'Where's Dad?' Hugh asked, coming in through the door. 'What's she snivelling about?'

'Dad's in his study, I think. And one of her cars has disappeared.'

'It was the pink one! Barbie's one!'

'Barbie's far too big to fit into that titchy little thing. Don't be stupid.'

'You don't know anything about it, by any chance?' Sally said, turning to her brother.

'Me?' Hugh exploded indignantly. 'What would I know about it? I don't play with her toys. I'm not a little kid any more. Do me a favour! I've got better things to do than stay here being accused of stuff. So, excuse me, I'll see you later.'

Sally had just about given up trying to get Bethan to eat anything when there was a knock at the back door.

'It's only me,' Edna Harding said as she came in. 'I came up to ask if you'd all like to come to lunch. Oh, dear. What's the matter?'

Bethan sniffed and hiccuped and stopped crying long

enough to tell her tale of woe. 'It was the one my dad gave me,' she finished, 'and I think the ghost's got it.'

'Why don't you come and have breakfast with me.' Edna eyed the mess. 'We'll see if the hens have laid any eggs, how about that?'

'OK.' Bethan slipped off her chair. 'I'll just get ready.'

'She's missing Mum,' Sally said when Bethan left the room. 'She and Hugh are in terribly grouchy moods this morning. I'm worried I can't cope, and with Dad going away tomorrow ...' Sally paused, threatening tears bringing a wobble to her voice.

'When I asked what the matter was, I didn't mean *her*.' Edna's face broke into well-worn lines round the mouth and eyes. 'I meant you.' She reached to pat the girl's hand. 'Don't worry. You aren't on your own. I'm here, aren't I? I'll help. I've brought up my own three – never mind six grandchildren.'

Sally wiped her eyes. 'That's really kind of you, Edna.'

'No trouble. I'll take her off your hands now.'

'But you've got the lunch to do.'

'She can help me. We'll be fine.'

Bethan went off with Edna, leaving Sally to sit at the kitchen table, sipping her coffee, trying to relax. Although she could manage for a while, playing mother to Bethan was not her favourite role; having the responsibility taken by someone else, someone more suited, was a major relief. Hugh was different. Last night had upset him, but so far this morning he'd shown no inclination to talk about it.

114

What had Dad said about teenage emotions causing psychic phenomena? 'Tell me about it,' Sally muttered as she washed up her coffee cup.

13

'There has to be someone in,' Sally said, knocking extra loud on Edna's front door.

'Why don't we try the back.' Hugh pointed to a small gate.

A blue brick path led round the side of the house, skirting the top of a good-sized garden. Roses, delphiniums and hollyhocks grew in profusion, colours vibrant against the green lawn. Herbs, near the kitchen door, gave off the scent of mint and thyme, and wide borders ran down to a well-ordered vegetable patch. Bean and pea sticks, rows of carrots and cabbages, reminded Sally of the miniature gardens at the Fête. Edna was coming up the path, a basket over one arm.

'Come in, come in.' She led the way through the back door. 'I don't use the front much. Make yourselves comfortable. Bethan's gone to get changed. She'll be down in a minute.'

'I'm coming now.' Heels clacked on the wooden stairs. 'Are you ready?'

Bethan had been transformed. Her hair, tied back in a neat bow, was smooth and shining. She was wearing a kilt and a white shirt, long socks and black patent leather shoes. Sally and Hugh watched her descent with open-mouthed astonishment. Bethan was absolutely delighted.

'What do you think?' Mrs Harding smiled up at her. 'Doesn't she look a picture?'

'Yes.' Sally nodded. 'She looks – very nice.'

'I've never seen her in a real dress.' Hugh grinned. 'She looks like a proper girl. She looks all right!'

'Belonged to my daughter's youngest, she's grown out of it. Might as well make use, it was only heading for the jumble. Dinner won't be long. Just waiting for the family to arrive. Jack and your dad are in the pub, but they know it's one o'clock sharp.' Edna waved Sally's offers of help away. 'Hope you're hungry.'

'More meat anyone?' Jack Harding held a bone-handled carving knife, the steel blade honed to a thin bow. 'Hugh?'

'Yes, please. Don't mind if I do.'

'How about a few more roast potatoes?' Will's mother edged the dish over.

'I wouldn't say no.' So far Hugh hadn't said 'no' to anything. Sally eyed her brother with distaste, the gravy was lapping over the edge of his plate. Not that it bothered anybody. The Hardings were hospitable, generous to a fault. Hearty eaters themselves, they liked to see healthy appetites.

'We never get dinners like this at home.' Hugh loaded his fork. 'Never, ever.'

Sally shot him another warning look.

'I was just saying!'

'I don't expect your mum gets a lot of time,' Will's mother said tactfully, 'what with a job and a family.'

'No, she doesn't,' Sally replied. 'This is a treat, I must admit. Thanks for inviting us.' She smiled at Will's gran. 'It's really excellent.'

'A pleasure, my dear. Would you like some wine? Elderflower, made it myself. Or cider?'

'Cider. Thank you.'

'Can you pour it, Jack? I got the rheumatics in my hand.'

'Sure, Ma.'

'Change in the weather. Told you.' Will smiled at Sally.

'Taking after old man Lawrence, eh?' Jack winked at his son as he topped their glasses up. 'You'll be dowsing next.'

'Dowsing?' Hugh looked up at Will. 'Can you do that?'

'No.' Will laughed. 'He's talking about my grandfather.'

'My dad was a dowser,' Will's mother explained. 'He could find water, and other things, too.'

'Like what?' Hugh asked.

'Damnedest thing I've ever seen,' Jack said. 'He was walking across Temple Field holding a rod of split hazel. You can't see nothing on the surface, just bumps. Suddenly the rod went down, twisting in his hands, he could hardly hold it.' He demonstrated, the muscles tensing, tendons standing out on his thick wrists.

'Which way did it go?' Philip Goodman asked.

'To the right, I think.'

'What's the difference, Dad?' Hugh laughed. 'Anyway, I

119

thought you didn't believe in things like that.'

'Left means water of some kind. Right means something else, perhaps a hidden structure. I said I didn't believe in psychic phenomena, ghosts and such,' he corrected his son. 'Dowsing is different. Clive Rowlands, the chap I'm going to see tomorrow, uses dowsers on his digs with very good results.'

'I'm with your dad on that,' Jack agreed. 'Saw it with my own eyes. I was just a little kid, but I'll never forget it. Rest of it, though – ghosts and that – I *don't* buy.'

'Not even at the Saracen's Head?' Philip inquired, mock-serious.

'Especially not there.' Jack roared with laughter. 'There are that many tales. All rubbish. Take old Bill Goodwin—'

'Has everybody finished?' Lyn Harding gave her husband a glare. These people had to live there. 'It's all nonsense, Jack. You just said that.'

'That's as maybe.' Jack's eyes gleamed. 'But it makes a good story.'

His wife looked round. All attention was on him, nothing would stop him now. 'Come on, Bethan.' She held her hand out to the little girl. 'You can help get pudding ready.'

'Old Bill Goodwin was the last landlord,' Jack began, 'and he reckoned he saw this knight—'

'I bought the place from him,' Philip recalled. 'Well, off his widow actually . . .'

'What knight?' Hugh interrupted, addressing Jack.

'It was round Christmas-time. Bill was down in the cellar, changing a barrel, and he reckons he saw a knight, all dressed in white, coming down the steps towards him – armour, sword, the full monty. He looks that real, old Bill thinks he's going to speak, but this knight just keeps on walking,' Jack slid one palm past the other, 'straight through the wall.'

'I heard that.' Will nodded. 'I told you . . .' he turned to Hugh. 'Are you all right?'

'Hugh?' Sally looked over as her brother's fork clattered on to his plate.

'Are you OK, son?' His father leaned towards him. 'Do you want to go outside?'

'No. I'll be fine. Just eaten a bit too much, that's all.'

'Anyway,' Jack went on, 'Bill comes steaming up those stairs, like all Hell is after him, and goes straight for the brandy. He's shaking that much, he can't keep the glass under the optic. One of the lads says, "What's up, Bill? Seen a ghost?" and Bill says, "How did you know? I just seen a knight, all dressed in white—". The lads collapsed. "Sure it weren't Henry VIII?" one of 'em says. "Or one of his wives?" Bill looks around, all bewildered, like.' Jack laughed loud at the memory. 'And the bar is full of people off to a fancy-dress party!'

'What about going through the wall, though?' Hugh said quietly. 'A real person couldn't do that.'

'What?' Jack's laughter wheezed to a stop.

Hugh repeated the question.

'Old Bill could have gone through walls himself, what with the booze he'd put away and the scare he'd had.'

'There's some that don't see it like that.' Edna Harding frowned.

'I know, Ma, but . . .' Jack shifted in his seat under her scrutiny. Suddenly he seemed about the same age as Hugh.

'But nothing. There's some think he *did* see something but you lot refused to believe him, and what with that, and all the teasing he got, it turned his mind, poor soul.'

'Now, Ma. There's no proof. The drink could have done that.'

'You shouldn't mock the afflicted.' His mother's mouth sealed to a tight, disapproving line. 'Nor the dead, for that matter.'

'He's dead, then? This man?'

'Oh, yes. Jack didn't tell you that exactly, did he? Spoil the story. He died down there, right in that cellar.'

'Of what?' Hugh's eyes widened in shock.

'Fell down the steps.' Jack Harding picked up a stick of celery. 'Neck snapped, just like that.'

'Jack!' His mother's frown deepened. 'There's no need for that kind of talk!'

'Sorry, Ma.' Jack helped himself to a hunk of cheddar and bit into the celery stalk. 'Some in the village say he took fright again, and it was too much for him. More likely he'd been at the brandy. He was drinking more than he sold by then. Place was going from bad to worse. Ghost or no ghost, his old lady didn't stick around. She sold up and got out pretty sharpish.' He laughed and looked at Philip. 'I bet the estate agent didn't tell you any of this when you bought the place.'

'No, he didn't.' Philip shook his head. 'But even if he had, it wouldn't have made any difference.'

After lunch was over, Jack and Philip retired to the lounge to finish their drinks, Will and Hugh went next door to look at Will's computer, taking Bethan with them, and Sally helped Lyn with the washing up.

'Give Edna a chance to put her feet up,' Lyn said, when they were in the kitchen. 'She's not getting any younger, but it's impossible to stop her doing things. She'll be offering to make Jack and your dad a cup of tea in a minute, you see if she isn't. Can't stay still for a second. She's hopeless.'

But Edna did not do that, not immediately. She settled in the rocker, eyes closed. The deep male voices soothed her. She listened for a while to the two men talking together, discussing Philip's plans to clear the cellar ready for this archaeology fellow, but her own thoughts came between what they were saying and she began to drift off.

She was glad Philip Goodman had bought the place. His name described him aptly, and he had kids to be proud of – Sally especially. Young Will seemed to have taken a shine to her. Edna smiled to herself; she'd seen the way the two of them looked at each other.

The old place needed a family living in it. That's what

Philip had in mind, even though his wife wasn't with him. Edna was old enough to know more than people told her on the surface. She'd seen it in his eyes the first time he'd come round to discuss the conversion with Jack.

The Saracen's Head wanted a change. A bit of real life; not the empty good spirits of the public bar. It had been going downhill for a long time, and it did have its dark side, there was no denying that. Over the years, the pub had suffered its full share of tragedy. Given the age of the building, that was hardly surprising and, according to Will, it was older, far older, than even she had imagined.

Poor old Bill Goodwin's fate was merely the last in a long line of accidents and untimely deaths which had scarred the history of the Saracen's Head. One in particular stuck with Edna. It had happened over fifty years ago, but still, even now, every so often, something would happen to remind her.

An old chap, he was. An antiquarian. A second-hand bookseller. He had a shop in town, poky little place – gone now, the whole area knocked down. What was his name? She could not remember for the life of her, but she could see him, white wispy hair, teeth like old piano keys; always immaculate, dressed in black with a wing collar, and that was considered old-fashioned, even in those days. He had been coming to the village every July/August time since the war, staying at the Saracen's for his annual holiday, and then that last year he killed himself.

Hanged himself in one of the rooms upstairs, he did, the

one next to the bathroom. Edna had been helping in the kitchen the day they found him. May Wells, who had gone upstairs to 'do', called the landlady, Agnes Odell, to his room. Edna could still hear the quake in the landlady's voice, see the shock, the fear, in both their faces when they came downstairs again. She could see May, the maid, homely little body, face as white as a flour dumpling, eyes huge with what she'd seen. May was fit for nothing, shaking so much she could hardly walk. It was Edna who had gone back with the landlady.

'There's something needs seeing to, before the police are called,' Agnes had said. 'I want someone I can trust, and I trust you, Edna.'

One glance was enough to show that the poor man was beyond earthly help, but what they found made Edna fear for his soul, then and ever after. What he'd been up to in that room did not bear thinking about. Books lay open. Strange symbols written on thick vellum pages. A pentagram, circled in salt, chalked into the carpet. Candles, burnt away to dribbling heaps of wax, stood next to devices designed to contact the dead. The landlady had gone round collecting it all up, scuffing out the chalk marks, spreading the salt with her foot. There would be enough of a scandal without this, and Agnes Odell was a superstitious woman.

Edna could see it all plain as day. She could remember the names of May Wells and Agnes Odell: both dead and gone now, poor souls, but she could not for the life of her remember his. It remained hidden from her. Funny how the memory played tricks. It bothered her when she couldn't recall something like this. That's how Alzheimer's started, and senility was something she dreaded. The man's name. What was it? It began with an initial. D. Two initials. D something. D. W.?

'Fancy making a cup of tea, Ma?' Her son broke her train of thought.

'Not for me, Mrs Harding.' Philip stood up. 'We've trespassed on your hospitality long enough. I'll collect the children and be off. Thank you for a wonderful lunch.'

She accompanied Philip to the door and, between the exchange of social pleasantries and making various plans, she forgot all about even trying to remember the name of that poor unfortunate man.

14

'Hugh? Are you OK?' Sally called, as she knocked on his door. She was worried about him. When they got back from Edna's he had gone straight to his room and hadn't been out of it since. He had still said nothing about what had happened the night before, but he'd gone a very funny colour at lunch, when Jack had started talking about ghosts. He'd been bad-tempered and snappy most of the day – a sure sign he was upset.

She had heard him clearing up the mess of milk and glass on the landing earlier. That in itself was completely out of character, as he had never voluntarily cleaned up anything before. Sally knocked again, harder this time. She did not intend to go away, whatever he said.

'What do you want?' the answer came back.

'Nothing. Dad's putting Bethan to bed. I just came to see what you are up to. Can I come in?'

Before he could stop her, Sally was in the room.

'I'm not up to anything.' Hugh sat cross-legged on the floor, leaning back, arms wide.

'Oh, yeah?' Sally looked straight at him. 'So what's that you're trying to hide?'

'Nothing!' Hugh tried adding indignation to his tone of innocence, but then the whole thing folded. 'Oh, all right,' he sighed. 'I could do with your help, to be honest, so you might as well see. It's that ouija thing I got from Will's mother. I've repaired it, painted in the damaged letters and numbers. This bit was missing, so I made a replacement. It's called a planchette.'

'What is?'

'This bit.' He pushed at a heart-shaped pointer cut from fresh wood. It ran backwards and forwards on little wheels.

'So *that*'s what happened to Bethan's car. Flakes of pink paint adhered to what remained of a mutilated chassis. 'That was a mean trick, Hugh!'

'OK, OK. I'll get her another.'

'When?'

'Whenever! I nicked one out of her toy box, flattened it out and stuck it on the bottom of this piece of wood. Good, eh?' Hugh spun the wheels, admiring his own ingenuity. 'Now it's ready to go.'

'How does it work?'

'Well, you put it on the board, like so . . .' He lightly placed the planchette, holding it steady with his fingertips. 'And it zooms up and down spelling things out. That's where you come in. I need someone to write down the messages.'

'What messages?'

'Messages from beyond the grave.' Hugh put on his special spooky voice, the one he used for scaring Bethan.

Sally stared at him, arms folded.

'You are not serious?'

'Of course I am—'

'Now look, Hugh.' She frowned down at him, unable to believe what he was proposing. 'Let's get real for a minute. Last night you were more frightened than I've ever seen you—' Hugh began to protest, but his sister put up her hand to quell him. 'No! Just listen! There's something going on here and we have no explanations, no control – you've felt it, I've felt it . . .'

'That's the point. Don't you see? We've got to get to the bottom of it and this might be the way to do it.'

'What if it isn't? What if that makes it worse? Goodness knows what might happen—'

'And what if it doesn't? You've got to help me, Sally.' He tapped the board nervously, mouth set in a stubborn line. 'If you won't – fine! I'll do it myself.'

He glared up at her, defiant. He would go ahead regardless, Sally could tell by his face. Whether she helped him or not . . .

'All right.' Sally sat down next to him. 'What do you want me to do?'

'Use this,' he said, handing her a pencil and pad, 'to take down any stuff that comes through.'

'Now what?'

'We ask.'

'Ask what?'

Hugh steadied his hand on the pointer. ' "Is there anybody there?", I guess.'

The toy wheels spun beneath his fingers. The heart-shaped piece of wood arced over the polished board, jerked back to compensate for a tiny overshoot, and landed up on 'YES'.

'Hugh!' Sally jumped so hard she snapped the end of her pencil. 'You're doing that yourself!'

Hugh was white, freckles standing out dark on his cheek, sweat beading his upper lip.

'I'm not, Sal. Honest to God.'

His fingers trembled but the pointer stayed steady on the board.

'Here it goes again!' He only just had time to warn her. Hugh shouted out the letters, trying to keep up with the speed of the planchette.

'W-H-A-T-D-O-Y-O-U-W-A-N-T? What do you want,' he repeated, just to make sure Sally had written it correctly.

'Ask who it is.'

'OK. Who are you?'

The pointer moved again, zipping backwards and forwards over the board.

'S-T-E-P-H-E-N. Stephen Who? D-E-B-A-N-V-I-L,' Hugh spelt out. 'Are you writing this down?'

'Debanvil? Oh, I see. Stephen de Banville. French, eh?' Sally looked at her brother, relief and anger vying inside her. 'Nice touch.' She put down the pencil and paper. 'That name is *really* fakey. You are having me on, aren't you?'

'I swear, I'm not.'

'Oh, right. Next thing you know, he'll say he's a Templar.'

The pointer moved across the board to 'YES' and stopped.

Sally searched Hugh's face for a hint in the eyes, any twitch in the mouth. If he was setting her up she would kill him. But there was no sign of it. Hugh was serious, his expression tense and focused.

Sally picked up the pencil. 'Ask him something else.'

'I've got a special question.'

'Go on, then.'

Hugh closed his eyes. 'What is happening here?'

'That's no good. It's too big, too vague.'

'The pointer's moving. Write this down and shut up, Sal.'

'What does it spell?' Hugh asked when the pointer stopped.

Sally looked at what she had written.

'S-E-C-R-E-E D-A-U-N-G-E-R. Could be secret danger, or dangerous secret.'

'What secret?' Hugh asked. 'What is dangerous about it?'

They hunched over the board, both tense now, staring at the pointer and completely absorbed.

'Sally? Hugh? Are you in there?' The knock at the door went through them like a jolt of electricity.

'Quick! It's Dad!' Hugh leapt up, kicking over a coffee cup. 'Oh, no!'

He looked in horror as the contents spilled on to a book

cover. It was one of the glossy numbers that Dad had lent him. He mopped at the mess with his sleeve, but brown liquid was seeping into the edges, making them stained and puckered, gluing them together.

'Never mind that!' Sally hissed. 'Get rid of this.' She pushed the ouija board towards him as the knock came again. 'Shove it under the bed or something.'

'Everything OK?'

'Fine,' Sally replied, and went to open the door.

'Have either of you been in my study?' her father asked as he came into the room.

'No.' Sally shook her head, as did Hugh.

'It's just somebody has. Things have been moved about,' he went on. 'Nothing's actually gone, but somebody logged on to the computer.'

'Didn't you lock up this morning?'

'Yes.' Philip frowned, perplexed. 'Or I thought I did.' He gave a rueful grin. 'I can be a bit absent-minded.'

'Are you going to call the police?' Sally asked.

'No.' Her father shook his head. 'Nothing's been taken. It could just have been kids. I don't want to make too much fuss about it.'

When he was getting ready for bed, Hugh thought about having a go with the ouija board on his own. He pulled it out ready, then pushed it back under his bed. When Sally was there it was different. On his own, shadows gathered. He remembered last night, and Jack's story about the white knight. He had a name now – Stephen de Banville. Maybe it was him that Hugh and the previous landlord saw. Jack could take the mickey, say it was someone in fancy dress, a case of mistaken identity, but Hugh knew different.

He had tried his hardest not to think about it, but it was there all the time, threatening his mind. He could see the thing begin to rise, forming from mist into a solid shape: a shimmering sequence of images, each one transparent but moving, merging, layering one on top of another, until they became something recognisable; a figure substantial enough for Hugh to see the sweep of the white cloak, with its cross staining the shoulder, and the chain glimmering, shifting like scales, on a mailed arm.

He had heard the ring of spurs on stone; had stood, frozen, terrified that it would turn and would see him, or worse, that it could *not* see, that bone and empty socket was all there would be. That was when the glass of milk left his hand, shattering on the ground. Cold liquid splashed up, chunks of glass hit his bare foot, and still Hugh could not move. He had watched, mesmerised, as the apparition began to break up, grow less solid again, then flow into the wall.

Maybe the ghost was this Stephen de Banville. Hugh remembered his hand, wrenched this way and that. He pushed the ouija board further under his bed, along with the planchette. Out of sight, out of mind: that worked most of the time. On the other hand, maybe he should get rid of it, like that head thing . . .

Although the inn sign was not in the room, Hugh could still feel the chill of its presence. He recalled something he'd read last night about Baphomet. Every preceptory had a representation of the idol. Maybe the tradition lived on and in this place the sign was it. Maybe he and Sally should have asked the ouija board. Perhaps not. Nausea came in a sickening wave, at the mere thought of it.

Hugh looked across the floor, his attention caught by something white on the carpet. It was a business card, heavily embossed with old-fashioned curly black print. He had never seen it before. It must have fallen out of one of the books Dad had lent him.

D. W. EWART

Antiquarian bookseller

2 Hobb's Passage

Off Moat Lane

Westbury

Westbury. That was the name of the local town. He could buy Dad a book to replace the one he had just wrecked. An antiquarian bookseller was bound to have the right kind. Hugh flicked the card and put it in his wallet. It would make a change to get out for a while. Maybe they could go tomorrow.

15

Tony Holt had worked far into the night, preparing himself for the task ahead. Now all was ready. The action would take place the following day. Holt found it hard to believe but, despite all his scholarship, Philip Goodman had no idea what lay hidden beneath his property, the Saracen's Head. By the time he found out it would be too late.

Goodman was going away. Garvin's little visit to the house had confirmed that. He had obtained, among other things, a copy of Goodman's schedule of meetings. Garvin had his uses. He had also planted a small bugging device, an initiative which had been rewarded almost immediately. Goodman had received a phone call which would require him to spend the night away. He would be absent for twenty-four hours at least, and that was all the time necessary.

Philip rose early. He planned to leave while his children were still asleep. He stood in the kitchen, drinking coffee, with no sense of threat, no premonition of the dangers gathering around his family. Out of the window, sunlight, diffused through leaden clouds, gave the sky a peculiar sheen like burnished pewter. The day was already warm and it wasn't even 6.30 a.m. He swilled his cup, picked up his brief-case, and went out to the car, his mind already on his plans for the day.

He was to see Rowlands, the archaeologist, at 9.00 a.m. and then had to get to London to meet with his publisher. He had cancelled his later appointments because he had a plane to meet, a flight into Heathrow, due in late afternoon, early evening. He smiled as he started the car. A phone call received last night; this meant he would have to stay overnight.

The children slept on after he left. There had been no strange occurrences that night in the Saracen's Head. Independently, without consulting each other, the children had devised their own way of buying peace. Bethan had dug out her oldest, most trusted cuddly toy, an ancient, battered, earless dog called Andy. He'd been in disgrace since Dad left, but now he was allowed back because he smelt of everything safe and happy. As long as he was with her, nothing nasty would happen.

In the bed opposite her, Sally wore the cross Will's mother had given her and, under her pillow, was a Gideon Bible she had discovered in the bedside cabinet. Hugh wore his Walkman, turned right down, to drown out any sounds, and slept with his fist curled round the snakestone he had retrieved from above the doorway.

Maybe it was these separate rituals and devices which secured tranquillity and a good night's sleep. Possibly. Or perhaps it was just that the house was waiting, making ready. Just like the night itself: the atmosphere was sticky, heavy with humidity, thick with electricity. Not one drop of rain fell, but that did not mean there was no storm coming.

Will began work prompt at 8.30 a.m. He wanted to take the van into town later. He had things to do, supplies to collect, but it was really an excuse to be with Sally. He planned to ask her if she would like to go, too, and if he made an early start, showed willing, his dad would be more inclined to let *him* go rather than one of the others. He'd been sent up to work in Bethan's old room. His job was to get at the electrical wiring by stripping the plaster off the wall. The floor was already covered in big chunks of the stuff, the air in the room thick with choking dust.

Will hardly noticed. He liked doing that sort of thing. It was satisfying stripping the layers away, peeling back all the modern additions and revealing the original features. Ripping the ceiling panels down, for instance, exposed the big old beams, restoring the room's natural proportions and showing how it used to look.

The hammer connected and the plaster hung for a second, held by a thin skin of wallpaper, before falling in sections and crashing to the floor. Will stepped over the jagged pieces and began pulling away the remaining patches to find the thick timbers underneath. Tie beams and braces. He stopped work for a moment, putting his sledgehammer aside to touch the pale brown wood. His architect's eye noted the pegged joints, and admired the skill that had gone into crafting a building which was seven hundred years old and still standing.

He shook his head slightly, his ears ringing in the sudden silence after the heavy hammer blows and falling plaster. He held his head cocked to one side, listening. No, it was not in his head. The sound was outside him; a kind of tinning. He thought it must be a radio downstairs turned up to distortion, but the lads always tuned into music stations and this sounded more like some kind of foreign language, the type you might pick up on a short-wave frequency. He went to the door and opened it. Nothing out there except KFM, the local radio station, faint from downstairs. He walked to the window and threw open the catch. Not out there either. It was coming from somewhere inside the room. He closed the window carefully, suddenly not wanting to look round.

Bethan's room was in the end gable facing over Temple Field. The wall was one metre thick, stone-built, the oldest wall in the house. Will stared out at the church, thinking about it and anything else, trying to ignore the sound behind him, pretending it wasn't happening. But it was growing louder, getting stronger, chanting in some unknown language. Harsh one minute, liquid and sibilant the next, it sounded Middle Eastern, like Arabic or Egyptian. He put a hand out to steady himself, grasping at one of the newly exposed beams. This was a wide crossbeam, a big forest timber. Will's fingers brushed against something which shifted away from him.

He jumped back, thoroughly spooked now. He stood on tiptoe but was not quite tall enough to see into the space beneath the eaves. Behind him the whispering seemed to intensify as he nerved himself to put his hand into the space and feel about. There was a box with what felt like a twig on top of it. Will's fingers closed around his find. The whispering stopped, like someone turning a radio off.

'There you are.' His gran came in carrying a tray of tea. 'I've been looking all over the place. What have you got there? What's the matter?'

She put the tray down. Something was wrong. Her eyes darted from his face, to the box, to the room itself. 'Let me see.'

Wordlessly, he handed his discoveries over to her.

'Where did you find them?'

'Up there in that alcove.' Will nodded towards the wall. 'The twig fell out of a nest, most likely.'

'Umm, maybe.' Edna Harding examined the withered slip of wood carefully. 'What's in the box?'

'I don't know. I've only just found it. I haven't had time to look.'

'It's light.'

Edna gave the old box a shake. The contents rattled.

Will's mouth went dry at the thought of what she might find, but finally he said, 'Open it.'

But before she could do so, Will's father's voice came roaring up from the floor below. 'Will! Where the bloody hell are you? I thought you wanted to take the van to town. If you don't get down here right now I'm sending somebody else.'

'I've got to go.' Will stripped off his overalls, dropping them in a heap on the floor.

'Do you want to take this?' She held the box out to him.

'No. You take care of it for me until I get back.'

She sat down on a shrouded chair. The box she held had once contained Havana cigars, but the thin cedar wood had warped and the paper covering was blotched and stained from having lain behind the plaster for many years. It had been hidden there deliberately, and for a reason, but why? Only one way to find out. Edna Harding looked down, her mouth compressed in determination. Her hand trembled slightly as she manoeuvred the box round, and her fingers suddenly went numb and clumsy as she tried to open the thin, tightly fitting lid.

The box's contents came under the general heading of personal effects. The long-ago contents of someone's pockets: a fob watch, a handful of old money, big heavy coins, a wad of dirty notes, green and red, held by a brass clip veined with verdigris. Edna unfolded a handkerchief with the embroidered monogram *D. W.* and underneath that was a newspaper cutting.

'Oh, I say,' she said, and one hand went to her mouth.

It was taken from a local paper, the *Herald* – the title had bitten the dust years ago, replaced by a jazzy tabloid – and the date at the top was 21 August 1956. She scanned down the page, shaking fingers smoothing the yellowing newsprint. She knew what she was looking for. The initials on the handkerchief, the date on the paper, had brought it all back: a small item, in the second column, right at the bottom. She groped in her overall pocket for her reading glasses. The print had almost worn off where the paper had been creased.

BOOKSHOP OWNER HANGS HIMSELF

Edna glanced at the first paragraph and then looked up, eyes drawn to the thick beam running across the ceiling. It had been in this room. The hook in the centre of the beam had been removed and the whole room redecorated, practically rebuilt.

SUICIDE: CORONER'S VERDICT

A local inquest heard how a Westbury bookseller was found hanged in one of the bedrooms of the Saracen's Head Hotel, Temple Marton.

A verdict of suicide while of unsound mind was returned on Mr David William Ewart, aged 65, who lived above the premises of his antiquarian bookshop in Hobb's Passage, off Moat Lane, Westbury.

The court heard how Mr Ewart checked into the Saracen's Head Hotel for a week's stay. Mrs Agnes Odell, wife of the proprietor, described him as 'a quiet gentleman who kept himself to himself', who seemed 'happy enough'.

She went on, however, to describe to the court how, the
following Friday, 1st August, he was found dead in his
room. Mr Ewart had, according to Mrs Odell, taken dinner
normally and retired early. He was discovered the next day
by the chambermaid, Miss May Wells, who had entered the
room for cleaning purposes.

'He seemed a very nice man,' Miss Wells told the court.
'It came as a terrible shock.'

'No one will ever know why Mr Ewart chose the
Saracen's Head Hotel,' commented the coroner, Mr Horace
King. 'He lived on his own and had no near family. Perhaps
these factors affected his state of mind at the time of his
death,' Mr King added before recording the verdict.

Local solicitors Powell, Smith & Powell are currently
trying to contact Mr Ewart's sister, a Mrs Virginia Holt. As
only surviving relative, a considerable estate is thought to
pass to her.

Edna sat on the edge of the chair, trying to relax her grip
on the paper. Suicide was a big thing in those days, a
disgrace, a crime even, not like now. The coroner always
tried to give an explanation. Not that he could ever guess
at the truth: the real reason this poor soul had done such a
terrible thing as to take his own life.

Edna thought back to when the body had been
discovered, turning her mind to the things found in the
room with him, things no Christian man should have had
in his possession. She had thought, assumed, they had all

been destroyed long ago but, just this morning, she had found one of them shoved under young Hugh's bed. The ouija board; instrument of the Devil. She had no idea how it had got there, how it had turned up again. It should have been got rid of long ago on the instructions of Mrs Odell. Edna seemed to hear the flutter of wicked things, like the rustle of bats' wings, the scrape of skin on skin, the sound of evil coming home to roost.

The twig Will had found on top of the box was rowan, mountain ash. She twirled the sprig of pale wood between her fingers. This belonged to a time of the old belief. It was a way of fighting like with like. Rowan was a powerful charm, used to protect against witchcraft, evil spirits. It had been placed on top of this box, with its pitiful collection of personal things, in the hope that it would still his restless spirit, banish any harm he might have left behind. Much good it had done. The magic had gone, withered like the berries it bore, the spell was broken. What would happen now?

16

Hugh had been keen to go with them, but he went off on his own as soon as they got to Westbury. Things to do, he said, but he promised Sally that he would be at the war memorial in Market Square by 12.00.

'What do you want to do?' Will asked.

'Just have a look round. You can show me the sights.'

'There's not a lot to see, to be honest,' Will said, as he parked the van.

The Market Square was a wide area right at the centre, even Hugh would not be able to miss it – it was the hub around which the whole town revolved. A large squat building made up one side of it. This had once been the butter market, but was now a museum. It seemed as good a starting point as any to get to know the place.

'I haven't been in there for years,' Will said as they went in. 'When you live somewhere, you don't, do you?'

The bottom floor was devoted to geology and dinosaurs. Sally made a mental note to bring Bethan. It would fill up a rainy day and she liked that kind of thing. Upstairs contained the history of the town, from earliest times until now. Sally was pressing buttons on an illuminated display when she heard Will call to her.

'Hey, Sally. Come over here and look at this.' He was

examining a long glass-topped cabinet full of all sorts of things, from flint arrowheads and Roman jewellery to medieval coins and weaponry. Will nudged her gaze upward.

THE WEBSTER COLLECTION

Montegue Webster, the noted antiquary, was a resident of this town from 1765 until his death in 1789.
He collected extensively in Britain, Italy, Greece and the Middle East, and was a keen local historian. Some of his finds from the town and surrounding area can be seen here.

Will was pointing to something lying at the back of the cabinet. A sword. Plain-hafted, long blade uncorroded, not nicked or pitted, it still held a dull sheen. Sally could see that it was beautifully crafted, although she knew nothing about weaponry.

'What a magnificent piece!' Will whistled in admiration. 'A weapon like that would have cost as much as a car. It would be like owning a BMW.'

'Yes,' Sally agreed. 'It's – lovely.' She hesitated, not quite sure if that was the right word. 'But I don't see—'

'Look underneath!'

Will indicated a small handwritten notice.

Sword. Medieval. Found at Temple Marton,
1789. By Montegue Webster.

Under that was another label.

Medieval lead seal.
Sigillum Templi *– the Seal of the Temple.*
Reverse side bears the name of
Stephen de Banvil.

Sally read the name again. Her heart felt squeezed, all of a sudden she found it hard to breathe. The label bore the name Montegue Webster and the date, 1789, but the actual object was missing. There was just a drawing of it.

'Where is it? The real one, I mean.' Sally wanted to see the actual thing. It was very important.

'Maybe it's on loan or something. We can soon find out.'

Will went off in search of an attendant and came back with an assistant curator. The name on her badge said *Caroline Stubbins.*

'What we want to know is', Will indicated the gap in the cabinet, 'what happened to this?'

'Oh.' The young woman blushed slightly and bit her lip. 'I'm afraid it's been stolen.'

'How?' Will looked up at the security cameras, the double lock on the cabinet.

'We had a gentleman, he said he was a numismatist, a coin collector. He asked to look at some of the coins. The cabinet was opened for him to examine them and then some time later it was noticed that the Templar Seal was missing. An attendant was with him at all times, of course,

147

watching like a hawk. But still,' she shrugged, 'we think he must have taken it.'

'Haven't you got him?' Will gestured at the cameras. 'On video.'

'Unfortunately not. There was some kind of interference: none of the images obtained on that particular afternoon are good enough to provide any kind of positive identification. Is there anything else? Is there some other way I can help you?'

'No. Thanks.'

'In that case—' The young woman was walking away when Will called out:

'Yes, there is. One other thing. When did this happen?'

'Oh, very recently.'

'How recently?'

'A week or so ago.'

'What did the guy look like? Do you know?'

'No.' The girl shook her head. 'I wasn't on duty, and the attendant who was with him isn't here today. The police have a full description, but the theft wasn't noticed for some time, so even if we did find him, it would be difficult to prove.'

'I see. Thanks for your help.'

'Any time. Enjoy your visit.'

The young woman went off to deal with another inquiry.

'What are you thinking?'

'I was wondering who took it and why,' Will replied, staring into the cabinet.

'Have you got a theory?'

'Maybe. I'll tell you after. Let's go and meet Hugh.'

Hugh was just about to give up his search for the bookshop. Every person he asked simply looked at him blankly or turned out to be a stranger like himself. The only Hobb's they knew was a Hobb's Way and that was a new road leading up to Sainsbury's. He was going to go back, conscious that time was against him, when he rounded a corner into a street he had not been in before. Moat Lane. There was a sign above the corner shop. The place he was looking for was off Moat Lane, the card had said.

The street was a mix of terrace houses and small shops which had seen better days – dusty windows with faded displays. The paving-stones beneath his feet were uneven and cracked. The whole area looked run-down. Hugh looked the length of the street, trying to assess whether it was worth going further. There was no one to ask. The street was deserted, very silent. There were no cars, no noise, not even a dog barking. He was just about to stop looking when he suddenly saw black letters on chipped enamel, *Hobb's Passage*, on the other side of the road.

There was no traffic about, but Hugh crossed on the zebra crossing. The orange globe on one of the Belisha beacons was broken, but the bulb inside winked obediently on and off. The entry on the other side of the road was easy to miss; just a narrow archway between two of the houses. The brickwork was crusted and dirty, old and crumbly, the roadway cobbled with a central gutter. It was more of a courtyard than a passageway. Buddleia and weeds grew from behind iron railings and up through gratings. One side seemed to be the backs of houses. The only shop was about halfway along.

Hugh approached the window. The books on display confirmed this was the right retail outlet. A lot of the volumes looked pretty old and musty, but there in the middle was his dad's latest. Hugh's heart skipped a beat. There, underneath it, was *Knights and Knighthood*, the book he was looking for, the book he had ruined. Hugh leaned forward to see if there was a price, his head right up against the glass, touching the scratched and peeling letters which read:

D. W. EWART
Antiquarian Bookseller
Good-quality antique and second-hand books

It was almost as if he was expected. Someone stirred inside and came over to the window. A hand reached in from the back and long bony fingers grasped the book that Hugh had been staring at.

Hugh heard the door ting. He looked up to see a face looming towards him, watery blue eyes blinking from under long wispy eyebrows. Straggly tufts of white hair stuck out around a skull the colour of polished ivory. Pale skin stretched latex-thin over sharp cheekbones and a high bridged nose. Bloodless lips drew back over teeth the colour of old piano keys. A voice came out, creaking and thin, and said, 'Won't you come in?'

17

Sally looked at her watch. She had positioned herself to see any approach to the Market Square, but there was no sign of Hugh. He should have arrived nearly an hour ago. He was not always on-the-dot punctual, but he was never this late. Will was being really good about it, but she could see he was anxious to get back.

'Maybe he got lost,' Will suggested, trying to stop her worrying. 'It's possible. After all, it is a strange town.'

'It's my fault.' Sally bit her lip. 'I shouldn't have let him go off. He acts so grown-up, I forget how young he is.'

'He's nearly thirteen. He can look after himself.' Will sighed, eyeing a prowling traffic warden. 'I have to move the van. If I get a ticket, Dad'll kill me.' Frowning, he put his hands in his pockets. 'I ought to get back. Dad's expecting me . . .'

'I know. Look. Don't feel you have to wait for us. You go. We'll get the bus.'

Sally paced to the end of the steps and back again. Her fears were dissolving, replaced by anger at her brother's total lack of thought. Hugh wasn't just putting *her* through it; there was Will, too. She stopped as a deeper resentment began to surface. He was getting out of line, taking

153

advantage – he wouldn't do this to Mum or Dad. First Bethan, with that performance yesterday morning, and now him. She couldn't control them. Sally felt tears starting. Why should she have to?

'Sal! Sally!' Suddenly Hugh was there, standing in front of her, hands on knees, trying to catch his breath, gasping out apologies.

'Sorry I'm late. I got caught up. I found – I found this place. An old bookshop with this strange old bloke in it—'

Will already had the engine started.

'Save it for later, Hugh. Just get in the van!'

'It was weird. Like he was expecting me. He had the book I wanted wrapped and ready. He even knew about Dad.' Hugh pulled out a second brown paper parcel. 'He gave me this for him.'

'How did he know him?' Sally asked.

'Dad's been there before.'

'Oh, yes.' Sally nodded. Something about coincidences, she remembered now.

'Where was it again?' Will asked, watching for traffic.

'Hobb's Passage.'

Will shook his head. 'Don't know it. Are you sure?'

'Yeah. D. W. Ewart, Antiquarian bookseller, Hobb's Passage. I remember exactly. I've got a card, here in my wallet . . . Hang on. I can't find it.' He patted pocket after pocket. 'Oh, no! I must have lost it.'

'No sweat. You can show me some other time.'

'I don't mean the card.' Hugh began another frantic search through his clothes. 'I mean, the wallet!'

'How much money did you have in it?' Sally was trying to remain calm.

'I don't know A bit. The stuff Mum gave me and Dad gave me a fiver last night—'

Sally groaned. 'That's more than thirty quid! God, Hugh. You are *so* careless. Will, stop the van. We'll have to go back and look for it.'

Will pulled into the side of the road. 'Now, let's not panic here. Maybe you dropped it in the bookshop; that's the logical place to start.' He took the street guide from the dashboard. 'What was the name again?'

'Hobb's Passage. I remember it was off Moat Lane.'

'That rings a bit of a bell.' Will opened the *A–Z*. 'Hobb's Way, Hobb's Walk. No Hobb's Passage. I've found Moat Lane . . .'

'It's OK.' Sally turned to him. 'We've delayed you enough. Just give us the map and drop us off. We'll find it.'

'It's no trouble.' Will gave her a wry smile. 'I'm already so late, a couple of minutes won't make any difference. Hand me the other map book, in the back of the glove compartment.'

Sally reached in between parking stickers and Snickers wrappers. The *A–Z* said *NEW Edition*, but the price underneath was 6/–. It was ancient, permanently curled from being thrust into pockets, its blue-and-red cover faded to grey and orange.

'Let's have a look. Ah, here we are.'

Will flicked to the page he wanted and bent the book back. Hobb's Passage was hard to find. It was in a maze of little streets ... Will found it and put his thumb on it. Then he picked up the other guide. *Revised 2006*. He found the same page, held it down, and looked from one to the other.

'That's strange ...'

'What is?'

Will turned the books so Hugh could see. As far as it was possible to tell, the whole area had been developed. Hugh looked slowly from one map and then back to the other. He leaned forward, gripping the edge of the books so tightly the covers began creasing. He couldn't believe it. The black warren of streets where he had just been walking had been replaced by a shopping mall.

'We could go and look anyway,' Will suggested. 'It isn't far. Maybe you slipped down a sidestreet and got confused.'

'This is Moat Lane.'

Hugh looked up at the name and had to agree, but he knew in his heart this was all wrong. The name was the same but nothing else was: the road was wider, the pavements tarmacked, there were different road signs, a pelican crossing and double yellow lines.

On the right-hand side, there was a break in the row. An arrow pointed towards a pedestrian way: Hobb's Walk.

'This isn't right.' Hugh frowned. 'It wasn't like this at all.'

'Well, let's go and see, shall we?'

Will and Sally crossed. Hugh followed, shaking his head. This was definitely the wrong place. It was all little giftshops, and stalls selling ice cream and Ben's Cookies.

Halfway along there was a shop, its name spelt out in gold and silver curling letters: *Mystic Experience*.

'Let's go in and ask,' Sally suggested.

'It's not the same place, I'm telling you,' Hugh insisted. He was feeling confused and a little bit scared now. 'How are they going to know?'

'Won't hurt. Come on.'

Will's head brushed some wind chimes as they entered the shop and the young woman behind the counter looked up from her book. A notice above her head read: *Please think of your Karma – Do not steal*. The glass display unit in front of her showed trays of crystals and tarot packs. The air was heavy with the scent of joss-sticks and incense. Wall shelves held different coloured candles, brass knick-knacks and hand-crafted earrings.

'Hi. Can I help you?'

The girl was dressed in black, her hair plaited and wrapped. Her rather broad nose was pierced and she wore so many earrings they jingled and shimmered as she moved her head. Sally had seen her before. She was the girl doing the face painting at Temple Marton Village Fête.

'Yeah. Well, maybe . . .' Will started to explain, as best he could, the place they were looking for, the mystery they

157

were trying to solve. The girl listened politely, but it was clear from the start that she did not have the first idea what he was talking about.

Hugh turned away and stared at the intricate patterns contained in some mystic mantra poster. The whole experience was making him sick with embarrassment. He felt extremely foolish. Sally and Will were going to think he made it up, but the truth was worse than that. He had been in the place. He had visited a bookshop which belonged to a different age, had been in a different place in time and space, and he had never even noticed.

Hugh had been in plenty of old bookshops with his dad. He was used to the dusty atmosphere, the musty smell. Lots of them looked as though they hadn't been touched or changed in an age, but a hundred little things should have told him. The quiet dark shop only had two modern books among all of the stock. The old black table for a desk, its surface scuffed and scratched; the postcard display, hand-coloured portraits, local scenes in sepia which Hugh had just thought were collectables. The little wooden drawer for a till. Receipt book, ledger, even a spike thing with notes stuck on it. No shop had things like that any more. Hugh had not given any of it a second thought.

Then there was the man himself: his clothes, his manner; his voice, creaky through lack of use, rustling like dry leaves. He had greeted Hugh as though he had been expecting him; almost as though he had been informed of his coming. What did he say? 'I thought someone was trying to get in touch with me.' Hugh thought he meant Dad – he had even looked round for a phone or fax. Hugh put his head against the glass of the cabinet display. He suddenly felt hot. It was only now that he thought of the ouija board. How could he have been so stupid?

'Sorry,' the girl was saying. 'Can't help you, I'm afraid.' She paused. 'Mr Holt probably could, but he's away just now.'

'Mr Holt?'

'Yes, this is his shop. He knows lots about local history and such. He's quite famous in his way, there's some of his books over there.' She indicated a shelf next to the counter. 'But, like I say, he's away. Working on a project.'

Tony Holt's books were prominently displayed. Published by a small specialist publishing house, the top copy was entitled *The Mystery of Modern Alchemy*. The cover showed a reconstruction of an alchemical laboratory, and the blurb on the back proclaimed:

Tony Holt links the ancient study of alchemy to modern day magic and sorcery in his continuing search for the ultimate source of power, the key to life itself.

Underneath was a photograph of the author: bearded, large dark eyes, long black hair swept straight back. Sally recognized him immediately, and so did Will.

Tony describes himself as a modern alchemist. He uses his knowledge as an astrologer and a psychic to carry on what he sees as the supreme quest . . .

'The secrets of the present are enshrined in the past,' Tony says. 'Absolute knowledge is out there just waiting to be rediscovered.'

'I'll take one,' Will said, handing the girl a couple of notes. 'No need to wrap it.'

He accepted his change and picked up his purchase. Will had his suspicions about Holt – this shop, the book, its subject matter, just went to confirm thoughts already forming. He had a feeling that Holt and Garvin had pulled that stunt at the museum, working it between them, stealing the Templar Seal for some kind of weird purpose of their own.

He turned round to see that Hugh and Sally were already outside. Even through the window, Hugh looked rough. The day was becoming oppressive, hot and humid. The shop was small and the atmosphere in there thick with the sickly smell of incense.

'Are you OK?' Sally was asking her brother. 'You've gone a funny colour.'

'I'll be fine.' Hugh touched his forehead. 'I've just got a bit of a headache. I want to get back. I want to look at the book the old man gave me.'

'Excuse me,' the girl from the shop called after them. 'Is this yours?' She was standing at the door waving something. 'I just found it. One of you must have dropped it.'

'It's mine,' Hugh just about managed to say. She was holding his wallet.

18

When they got back, the battered yellow skip outside the pub was piled high with barrels and all sorts of rubbish from the cellar. Edna Harding was supervising one last deposit. The skip carrier was due any minute.

'What are you doing, Gran?' Will shouted out as he got out of the van. 'Hugh wanted that!'

His grandmother did not look at him as she directed two of the men to throw the inn sign up on to the very top. It leaned over slightly, the face looking down at her. She smiled back.

'If he wants it so much, how come I found it wrapped round with blankets and shoved behind a chest of drawers? Better off without it. Ain't a pub any more, is it? By the by,' she reached into her overall pocket for the cigar box, 'you found it, so it's yours. But if you want my advice you'll lob it straight up there with the rest of the rubbish. Oh, and your dad's looking for you.'

'Has Bethan been all right?' Sally asked.

'Been a little love. She's with me in the kitchen.'

'Sally, look at this.' Will had opened the box and was examining the newspaper article. 'Where's Hugh? He ought to see it, too.'

★ ★ ★

'And you reckon this is the man you met in the bookshop? How can it be?' Sally shook her head, and began to read the report on Ewart's suicide again. 'I don't understand.'

'Neither do I,' Hugh replied. 'But it is. The name was on the card, the window of the shop. It has to be the same one.'

'It can't be.' Sally checked the date at the top of the paper. 'This is dated 1956. Maybe it was his son, or nephew . . .'

'I don't think so. The shop was in a place which no longer exists. And it was old, but not like a museum, not in a state of preservation.' He paused, it was difficult to find the words for what he meant. 'It was old but functioning, like things must have been in those days. It has to be the same man. I can't think of any other explanation.'

Sally had to agree, however unlikely it seemed. The proof was in front of her and, whatever else he was, she knew her brother was not a real liar, but still it made no sense to her. This man was dead. He had hung himself in 1956, so how could Hugh walk into his shop fifty years later? She was about to ask him again, but he was still clearly shaken by the experience, it would do no good to question him further. She turned to Will instead – maybe he could come up with some kind of explanation.

The older boy frowned, and stared at the newspaper in her hand.

'Could be a time-slip,' he said. 'I read about it in one of those paranormal magazines.'

'You mean it's happened to other people?'

Some of the anxiety left Hugh's face at the thought that he was not alone in this.

'Yes. Lots of times. Well-documented cases. One thing I remember reading, one thing they all had in common, was a quality of profound silence throughout the whole experience.'

'Hey!' Hugh's blue eyes cleared even more. He gave a wide grin – almost back to his old self again. 'That's how it was for me! I remember thinking how quiet it was, no traffic noise, nothing! Did it, the thing you read, did it say why it happened?'

'Sometimes for no reason. Someone leans on a particular stone, or stands on a particular spot, and suddenly finds that they are back in the past.' Will shrugged. 'Other times, it could be an intervention; someone from the past giving a warning about something about to happen in the present.'

'Like what?' Hugh's anxiety started coming back.

'I don't know. Let's have a look at that parcel he gave you.' He held out his hand to Hugh. 'Maybe that will give us a clue.'

Before Hugh could hand the parcel over, Will's father came storming towards them. 'Where the hell have you been? When I ask you to get something I want it now, not next week—'

'Hang on, Dad—'

'Hang on, nothing! Where's the stuff? The cable and that? The list I gave you.'

165

Will looked up, eyes wide.

'You don't mean you forgot!'

'I was going to pick it up on the way back. I'll go now. Sorry, Dad. Sally? Hugh? I'll see you later—'

The book wrapped in brown paper was leather-bound and old. It looked similar to the one Philip Goodman had obtained from the same supplier. This volume was handwritten by the same man, Montegue Webster. His name was on the frontispiece in faded ink.

Montegue Webster
his Journal

'Let the past speak to the present'

The pages were stiff, the writing difficult to read. It was the last volume of his diaries.

'Come on. Let's go to Dad's study.' Sally shut the book. 'It'll be quieter there. We need to look at this really carefully. We have to try and work out exactly what's going on.'

Jack Harding was down in the cellar, filling in time while he waited for Will to collect the electrical equipment. His anger at his son's forgetfulness was not serious. Given a nice day, and a girl as pretty as that, the last thing on *his* mind would have been ring mains and junction boxes. He smiled. He'd been just the same at Will's age. Not that he'd ever let the lad know that – he was still in for a roasting when he finally got back.

Jack looked round the cleared cellar. He wasn't that annoyed because this was a job that needed doing. He'd been wanting to get down here, now the work was progressing well upstairs, to check for damp, to check the load-bearing capacity. Not that there would be much problem with that. He patted the wall by his side: solid stone. Damp was a different matter. It could play havoc in a building like this, creeping through stone, rotting the great supporting timbers. Medieval builders didn't know about damp courses, and the owners in recent years had paid more heed to tarting the place up than securing the fabric.

The cellar was a big space separated by dividing walls into different rooms and alcoves. Some were brick, others were much older, stone-arched, tunnel-like, clearly part of the original structure. Jack made his way through the brick and stone labyrinth, heading for the far side of the cellar to the oldest, thickest wall of all.

His lads had found a deal of stuff in this area: crates and barrels heaped up into a rickety pyramid. It was almost as though the things had been piled deliberately to form some kind of barricade. Perhaps Bill Goodwin had put them there. He remembered the old landlord's shaky hands, his red-rimmed panicky stare. Maybe the stories were right. Maybe he had taken fright and then missed his footing on the steep slippery steps, as he ran in headlong flight from something in the cellar. Jack glanced back towards the stairs, to the place where Bill had fallen, where they had found him, and rubbed at the gooseflesh suddenly travelling up his arms and rippling the golden hairs. It was cold down here. But that was how it was supposed to be. It was a cellar, after all. It made a change from the stifling humidity of the day upstairs. He grinned at his own sudden rush of fear. He was getting as bad as Mother.

Jack Harding surveyed the expanse of whitewashed stone that had lain behind the improvised barrier, running his hands along, checking for damp. There were little machines you could get nowadays to do the job for you, but he preferred to go by his own senses. Towards the far end of the wall, he stopped. There was an archway here, but it was not obvious at first glance. Layer upon layer of whitewash, applied regularly over centuries, had painted over and obscured the difference between the infill and the architrave.

He reached in his pocket, took out a penknife and began to scrape where the margins seemed to lie. Big white flakes, the size of A4 sheets, fell away to expose small blocks of dressed stone. They formed a low arch, squat and barrel-shaped. Jack was familiar with the history, the various phases of building and would have dated it, tentatively, as being twelfth-century. The space between was a different matter: this was blocked up, not by stone, but by brickwork. Jack scraped some more. The bricks were smaller than modern ones, not ancient, probably more like eighteenth-century. They had been crumbling away ever since beneath this thick sealing layer of caked lime.

He prodded tentatively at one of them and there was a shower of red dust as it shifted under his touch. He began picking away more whitewash to get at the bricks underneath. The mortar was soft and crumbling. He wanted to know what was behind, hoping he wasn't going to find huge great mushrooms of damp. He jabbed his knife into the rotting cement and went right through into some kind of cavity. The wall was bulgy and wobbly, built up in a single skin, probably. One good push and the lot would go. He began to ease one brick out, and then another . . .

'Bloody hell!'

He swore out loud and leapt back as something tumbled out. Jack Harding was not a squeamish man but his face tightened with disgust at what he had seen. Patches of black stuck in tufts to parchment skin punctured by a delicate fluted rack of white bone ribs. Huge eye sockets, empty and blind, stared from a skull laid back across the spine. Skeletal remains of a creature frozen in a final moment of terror and agony – canines snarling futile defiance, jaws gaping wide – fell at his feet.

'What is it, Dad?' Will had come down to the cellar to look for his father. He came running when he heard him shout.

'It's a cat. Some heartless bugger must've put him in

there. Poor little devil. Can you imagine that?' He toed the mess of bones and fur with his boot. 'I don't care what your gran says,' he added, 'there's no way I'm putting that back.'

19

The circumstances that led to this deliberate act of cruelty were described in the last words the distinguished historian, Montegue Webster, ever wrote. The last entries in his diary read:

July 26th, 1789

I arrived in Temple Marton, to find work well under way on the restoration of the Church. Lady Fitzpatrick, with whom I again have the honour of staying, is making a commendable effort to restore this ancient and beautiful structure, but my attention is drawn, yet again, to the Inn. My theory is that this place acted as the living quarters of the Templar Knights during their sojourn in Temple Marton. Her Ladyship knows of my interest in the Order and is willing for me to undertake further study of the building which comprises part of her estate.

July 27th, 1789

Getting the co-operation of the landlord is a different matter. He has a surly manner and is not inclined to have the old place 'messed about with'. I cannot see his objection: it is the cellar I wish to visit and this is, at present, a rat's nest repository for every kind of broken and useless object. He is a lazy, idle fellow who cannot bestir himself to clear the cellar out. His Inn is like himself, ill-kept and unsavoury. I say as much to her Ladyship, but she is of a different opinion. She tells me that the natives hereabouts are a primitive, superstitious lot.

The landlord and the other villagers are willing to believe all kinds of stories regarding the Inn. Foremost among these is a tale concerning a white knight, seen not only at night, but in the day as well. They have a very great terror of this spectre which is, by all accounts, very fearsome. They seem to believe him to be some kind of guardian spirit, hence their dread of any disturbance to the fabric of the building.

I listened with rapt attention as this story was recounted to me by one of the servants at the Manor. My excitement is aroused not by any belief in the supernatural on my part; no, it is because I feel I have uncovered something far more important. This story has been handed down through the generations, from father to son and mother to daughter. The truth has been lost in the constant retelling but it speaks to me of a time when Knights of the Temple were resident in this village.

July 28th, 1789

At last work has started in the cellars of the Saracen's Head. The landlord's co-operation was secured by golden guineas and a couple of sturdy fellows from the Hall are now employed in clearing divers accumulations of rubbish. The far wall looks most promising. The stone work there resembles that found in the crypt of the Church and may prove my theory that there is a connecting tunnel reaching under Temple Field.

July 29th, 1789

Work proceeding well. My goal is to find the Chapter House, the chamber which the Knights would have used for their meetings and perhaps for acts of worship. I have found what looks like an archway which is, at present, blocked. Tomorrow we will be ready to breach the wall and see what lies beyond.

July 30th, 1789

Work has progressed well; in fact we have found rather more than I had bargained for. The archway was cleared of all obstructing stone by late afternoon. It leads into a tunnel of very fine construction. I ordered torches lit, and was about to enter, when one of the workmen cried out. His eyes are young, quicker to adjust to the smoky flickering light. He caught my arm and held me back. Whey-faced and gibbering, I thought at first the man was raving. Then I looked down and saw the cause of his distress.

We had made a gruesome discovery. Human remains, curled on the floor. Was the poor unfortunate deliberately interred? Walled up alive in there? It is possible. I have heard of this in other places, as punishment for Knights who transgressed or betrayed the Rule. I could tell by what remained of his habiliments, the rags and fragments which had escaped the ravages of rat, rot and rust, that he was a Templar. Perhaps the villagers were not so far from the truth in their legend of a knight left to guard the place. Certainly they were much occupied now with making signs against evil and crossing themselves, despite my assurance that the bones at their feet had no power to hurt them.

I ordered the remains removed – we can at least give the poor soul a Christian burial. We have no way of telling his name, history or the way he came by his death. His grave site will be as anonymous as those of his Brother Knights who already sleep in the churchyard.

After his bones were removed, certain articles were found. I have spent the evening sketching them and will add them to my collection of curiosities.

July 31st, 1789

Early morning. I cannot sleep or contain my impatience. I returned to the Inn to inspect the chamber we found earlier in the day. It turns out to be a passageway, leading to a further room. This, too, is blocked off by stone. I must confess that, in the flickers of the torchlight, I too was infected by fear and superstitious dread of the place. Even here, back at the Hall, I shiver as I write and feel the small hairs rise. Perhaps these feelings will lessen with daylight. While I was there, I made another discovery. Masons' tools, scattered on the floor, inside the blind passageway. The presence of these instruments would suggest that the unfortunate Knight was responsible for his own demise, that he sealed himself inside. This is, indeed, a very great mystery.

July 31st, 1789

Evening. It took me all day to secure labourers willing to continue the excavation, and have had to distribute a deal of money, but I am determined that work will continue with the minimum of delay.

I will not be able to sleep again tonight. I am consumed with restlessness. I must know what lies within that second chamber!

The entries finished here. On the last page, a different hand noted:

Montegue Webster was found in the cellars of the Saracen's Head, having risen early to further the excavation on his own. Although seemingly robust and in good health, this excess of vigour proved too much for his constitution. He appears to have suffered an apoplectic fit and subsequently died of a brain fever without regaining consciousness. All work was stopped and the chamber sealed on my orders.

E. M. Fitzpatrick

'There must be some sort of secret chamber, in the cellar.' Hugh kept his voice low, almost whispering, as though they might be overheard. 'What do you think, Sal? Maybe we ought to go and check it out.'

Sally shook her head.

'Not yet. There might be workmen still down there. Go and see if Will's back. I want him to look at this.'

Their father's study was airless and stuffy. Sally followed Hugh outside and settled herself at one of the picnic benches. The yard was still. There was not a breath of wind and the atmosphere was hot and humid. The sky was clear overhead but purple clouds were crowding in from the horizon. Thunder rumbled in the distance. The little black bugs were out again. Sally brushed them from her vest.

Bethan was playing, but she did not bother Sally. She was busy with the car Hugh had bought her, running it along, on and off the tables, completely absorbed in her own little world. Suddenly she froze, car poised in midair, staring at the bench, watching her own shadow being swallowed up by another much bigger one.

'Hello, there.'

'Oh, hello.'

Bethan turned round and Sally looked up, alerted by the recognition in her sister's voice.

'You're the magician man!' Bethan exclaimed. 'Got any tricks for me?'

'Not today,' he said, and smiled.

He wore the same leather jacket, and the same smile that did not quite reach his eyes.

'Garvin's the name. Mark Garvin. Remember?'

Sally put the book down. 'Yes, I do. Can I help you?'

'Maybe.' His eyes darted to the volume in front of Sally. His hand reached out to caress the skin of the cover. 'That looks old. I'm a bit of an expert, a bit of a collector. Can I see?'

'It belongs to my dad.'

She put out her own hand to guard the book, but he had already taken it off the table.

'Mm. Very unusual. Handwritten.' He flicked to the back, eyes scanning the final entries. Only the slightest tremor betrayed the fact that his was anything more than a casual interest. 'I can give you a good price for it.'

'Like I said, it belongs to my dad. It's not for sale.'

'Pity.'

He held it for a second or two longer before giving it back to her. 'Where did he get it, if you don't mind me asking?'

'I – I don't know. You'd have to ask him.'

'Maybe I will. Is he about?'

'No. He's not here at the moment.'

'He won't be back till tomorrow,' Bethan chirped up.

Sally stared at her. That was the first she'd heard of it. 'How do you know that?'

Bethan ran the little car up and down the bench in front of her. 'He just phoned to say. We're staying with Edna tonight. She sent me to tell you . . .'

Her voice trailed away and she bit her lip. She had meant to come and tell right away, but somehow she'd got playing and forgotten all about it. Now Sally was cross, Bethan could tell by her face.

'Never mind. Can't be helped. We all forget things now and again.' Garvin grinned down at Bethan.

Sally glared. What had it got to do with him? Behind her back came the whirr and chatter of the fax machine.

'Maybe that's him now.' He jerked his head towards the office. 'Aren't you going to see?'

Sally stood up, expecting him to take the hint and leave. But he didn't. Instead he held up his camera.

'Do you mind if I take a few snaps while I'm here?' He took off the lens cap and began adjusting the focus. 'This pub is very old. Interesting history, so I believe—'

'It's not a pub any more,' Sally interrupted. 'It's a private house.'

'I know that. But it has got quite a story behind it. You can't really keep that kind of thing to yourself.' He aimed the camera at the back of the building and began firing shots on automatic. 'Do you mind?'

'Yes, I do.'

Sally scowled. He was making her feel uncomfortable. Her first impression, formed at the Fête, came back even stronger. There was something about him she did not like.

'Maybe some other time. When your dad's back, eh?'

Sally turned away from him to go into the office.

'Take care of that book now.' He picked it up and held it out. 'You don't want the rain damaging it.'

As she looked back at him, a spot of rain, the size of a five pence piece, splashed on to her neck. Distant lightning flickered like a filament behind his leather shoulder. His eyes held hers for a moment and then he turned to go.

'I'll be seeing you,' he said as he walked away. 'Bye for now.'

'Bethan, you better go in, it's starting to rain.'

'I want to stay with you!'

'I said go in!' Sally snapped. The encounter with Garvin had unsettled her. 'You'd better go to Edna,' she said in a calmer voice, trying not to take it out on Bethan. 'Get your things ready.'

The fax in the office was not from Dad. It was from:

Aubrey College, Archaeology Dept, Dean's Way, Sandingham

FACSIMILE

To: *Mr Philip Goodman, Saracen's Head, Temple Marton, nr Westbury*
From: *Clive Rowlands*
Time: *17.30 p.m.*

Dear Philip
Think I might have solved the riddle of the mystery slates.

You were right. Some of the symbols are alchemical. After you left, I had a chat with a friend of mine in Social Anthropology. He specializes in Cults and came up with an interesting theory as to the function of these plates and what they are doing dotted around the place.

He thinks they are the work of a modern alchemist; the man probably dabbles in other kinds of magic, too — of what hue I leave up to your imagination. My colleague thinks that these pieces of slate are markers, placed deliberately to locate and isolate a source of power. I know what you are thinking, but my colleague reminds me that some people take it seriously. Deadly seriously. I'm not saying this guy is dangerous, but forewarned is forearmed — if your alchemist is targeting the Saracen's — so expect a visit!

Hope this reaches you. I tried to get you at your publisher but you had already gone.

My colleague thinks there might be more markers out there, so get looking!

Sally stood up. The others needed to see this. They could scout round, see if more of these plates could be found. Thunder rolled outside, and single raindrops splashed on the window. Sally hoped the storm would hold off until they'd had a chance to search. Afterwards, they could go through the Montegue Webster document. The two things were connected in a way she did not understand. She started up in alarm — where *was* the book? She was sure she had put it down next to the fax machine, but it was not there now. Sally looked round frantically, searching through the mess of papers on the desk, and then realized it must be outside. The rain would ruin it. She ran to the door, but could see clearly that the table where she'd been sitting was empty.

Garvin said something as he got into the driver's seat and his companion nodded. The news that Philip Goodman would not return that night was merely information.

He held out a pale fleshy hand for the book. His long nails lightly scored the calfskin binding of Montegue Webster's journal, the pads of his fingers pressing down as if he could absorb the contents through the cover. The last entries confirmed long-held suspicions. Webster had died, or been killed, at the final stage in his quest to solve the mystery of the Templars. He had perished, his destiny unfulfilled, and the chamber had been resealed. Its secret was still there, waiting – for him. Holt's pale face became blank of expression, his black eyes stared at the rain spotting the windscreen and the sweeping wipers, but they saw nothing.

The driver knew better than to talk to him when he went into these kind of states. Garvin had his own powers but they were mean and small – simply not in the same league as those of his companion. Garvin could act on people's minds, using low-level hypnosis, causing sudden brief mental lapses, faults in the memory, like with the girl back at the pub. This, combined with quicksilver sleight of hand, made for a convincing magic act, but his companion was a magician of quite a different order: a powerful psychic, a modern alchemist, a practitioner of long-forgotten arts. Sceptics, scholars, scientists might scoff, but the driver did not. He had seen these powers in action.

Lightning flickered on the far hills; thunder rolled the storm nearer. This storm was no accidental meeting of weather fronts. It had been planned and timed, brought down upon them by the man sitting next to him. He could already create electrical disturbances, interfere with the natural workings of the world around him. The force he was preparing to take into himself tonight would give him power beyond human imagining.

Garvin tucked the car under overhanging trees, within sight of the pub. All they had to do was wait until the building was dark, deserted and shut off from the rest of the world by the driving rain.

His companion sat, eyes closed, the object of power absorbing all his attention. It had taken years of painstaking research in the libraries of France, Spain and Egypt to substantiate the existence of this, the Templars' most guarded secret – to verify its journey from the Middle East, to Cyprus, then Paris, and finally to this small obscure English village. Events had taken an unexpected turn when Philip Goodman acquired the property, but that was now only a minor inconvenience. Things were back on course. Within hours all Holt's efforts would be rewarded. He would succeed where others had tried and failed. Montegue Webster had neglected to take the right precautions and had been struck down by forces beyond his understanding. Uncle David had been on the right lines, but he had followed the wrong path, one bending to the right, leading towards the light. That was his mistake. Holt practised magic of a dark and sinister kind, in accord with the thing he sought to find. He was not about to make the same mistakes.

He could feel the vibration rising towards him, whispering invitation through layer on layer of earth, time, consciousness. It was waiting for him, he would be the instrument of liberation. It had waited, imprisoned for centuries – transmuting and refining, subjecting ancient knowledge to endless distillation – and now the process was over. In the quiet darkness of the hidden chamber lay the secret of secrets, the power to control all nature, the key to life itself.

A slip of paper lay on the floor. It must have fallen from the book Holt had been at such pains to obtain. While the rain drove against the windscreen and his companion sat lost in trance, Garvin picked up the note and read it.

I approach the last stage of my investigation into the mystery of the Templars.

The tiny neat writing went on to say:

If, along the way, I have been forced to resort to unorthodox measures, may the Lord God forgive me. May He protect me in this, the final part of my quest and, if I fail, may He offer His protection to others who might come after me.

D. W. Ewart

Garvin felt a flutter of misgiving. He knew the story of how Holt's uncle had taken his own life, his mind torn apart by what he sought to know. Holt maintained he was not making the same mistakes, but what if he was wrong? What if this thing was too strong? How many lives had it claimed? How many more would die in order for the Knights to keep their secret?

20

Hugh went out armed with a trowel and trailing a bin-bag, as though he'd been sent to clear weeds and trash. The burst of rain had stopped as suddenly as it had started. The sun was out again, but dark clouds all around promised to choke its rays at any moment. Spirals of steam rose from the buckled tarmac as Hugh worked his way round the building. His progress was slow and methodical: he stopped every now and then to stow rubbish or root up this and that. When he had finished, he slung the bag up into the new empty skip and went back into the house.

'Where's Sally?' Hugh asked.

'Gone to Gran's. Bethan was scared of the thunder, and wouldn't leave without her. She'll be back shortly.' Will looked up expectantly. 'Did you find anything?'

Hugh had found four slate tablets. Two had been in the earth for a while, long enough to become encrusted with deposits and silvered by snail tracks. The other two were unstained; put down to replace the ones he and Will had removed.

He put the pieces of grey stone side by side. Will stood behind him, staring down at the slim rectangular tablets, studying the mysterious scratched patterning of signs and sigils. He reached over and rearranged them into a diamond shape.

'Show me where you found them,' he said, bringing up a ground plan of the inn on the computer.

'Front window. Top corner. Far corner. And about here, at the rear.'

At each location, Will clicked in a little marker.

'I see,' he said, folding his arms and staring at the screen.

'I don't,' Hugh said, looking over his shoulder.

'OK. This shows the north/south orientation.' Will blocked off and removed the directional pointers from the corner of the plan, enlarging them and superimposing them on the building itself. 'Cardinal points of the compass. The arrows align with the markers.'

'Oh, yeah! Right!' Hugh sat down.

'OK. Let's try something else.' Will brought up a map of the village, enlarging the centre until the pub, church and Temple Field filled the screen. 'The Saracen's Head is aligned with the church, the two buildings are parallel. Now . . .' His finger hovered for a moment, then he hit a key. 'Bingo!'

Thin red lines appeared on the screen, describing the outline of a pentacle.

Hugh stared, eyes wide. 'How did you get that?'

'I've been out doing a bit of scouting of my own. I found two markers at either end of the church, and another here,' Will tapped the screen, 'at the base of the big boundary oak at the bottom of Temple Field. They connect with the ones on the side of the pub to make the pentacle. Now, the pentacle is a mystic symbol, but not just that. See here, in the middle, we have a five-sided shape. I am willing to bet that marks the position of a hidden chamber, under Temple Field. It probably formed part of the original preceptory.'

The chapterhouse!' Hugh exclaimed. 'The meeting place, built underground for the Templars' secret ceremonies.'

'Exactly. There ought to be one, and we have never found it. If it exists, it would be here under Temple Field, accessed via the archway my dad has just found in the cellar.'

'All right.' Hugh studied the slates again. 'But what are all these signs and funny squiggles?'

'The symbols were called sigils and they were used to write spells. It's all here. In Holt's book.' Will picked it up and showed Hugh the cover. 'I was having a read of it this afternoon, while I was waiting at the electrical suppliers. There's a whole section about the Templars. How they picked up some kind of secret knowledge in the Middle East. Only a few of them knew about it – a sect within a sect, if you like – and the Templars operated on a strictly "need to know" basis.'

'What was it?' Hugh asked, suddenly remembering the words spelt out by the planchette. 'What was the secret?'

'Holt's not going to give that away, is he? It would spoil the mystery. Holt's theory seems to be that the only thing that could have given the Templars their fabulous wealth and power was alchemy. They cracked it, in other words, found the secret the alchemists were searching for – ways to turn base metal, lead and such, into gold – that gave them their unlimited wealth. Alchemists were also looking for an elixir to give eternal life, ways to create living matter out of inorganic substances, outside the normal biological processes. Holt's thesis seems to be that the Templars found just that and that is why their activities were considered "unholy" – usurping the power of God, you see? That's why they were persecuted. But they spirited the thing away, right from under the French king's nose and hid it somewhere.'

Will lapsed into silence. Then he said, quietly, almost to himself, 'What if such a thing existed? If there was such a secret?' He spread his hands. 'If it worked then, why not now? If you take off the alchemy label – take it out of the medieval, all the spells and stuff and mumbo jumbo – what you get is the power to change atomic structure; to extend and create life. It could make modern particle physics and genetic engineering look like old-style alchemy. Whoever found it could control everything . . .'

Hugh nodded. He understood. What had been preserved at such cost, and hidden at such risk, could well be here. Not treasure in the normal sense. It could save and destroy, it had the power to make riches, make the trees flower, the land germinate. All the things attributed to the miraculous head – to Baphomet. That, indeed, was a dangerous secret.

Rain was falling heavily as the two boys went off to find Sally. She would be at Gran's house, or they would meet her on the way. In between looking out for her, and trying to avoid a soaking, neither of them noticed the car parked under twin horse chestnut trees just up the road from the Saracen's Head.

'Something has happened.' The eyes of the man in the passenger seat blinked open. 'The markers have been removed.'

'Can't they be replaced?'

'No. It's too late for that. We have to act.'

'When?' the driver asked.

'Now. As soon as possible. The tablets act as gates, controlling and channelling the psychic energy. Without them the whole site will become increasingly unstable. Has everyone left?'

'Yes.' The driver started the car. 'The two lads just went past. Jack and his boys knocked off half an hour since – they'll be in the pub by now – and the girl and her younger sister left some time ago with the old lady.'

'Do we have all the necessary equipment?'

'Yes.' The driver jerked his head. 'It's all in the back.'

'Very well, then. Let's get on with it.'

21

Sally had to wait for the rain to ease before leaving Edna's house. The old lady would not hear of her going out. Even after the downpour had stopped, she insisted on her taking an umbrella and suggested she go the back way, just in case the weather started up again. The alley was perfectly safe this time of night – quicker and more sheltered.

Sally had expected to find Hugh and Will in her dad's study, but when she got into the yard the room was dark and the door locked. The rain had diminished to occasional drops, but these were heavy, splashy, and thunder still growled low and ominous. The clouds hung down, purple indigo shading to blackness, like inky duvets.

Sally opened the back door. The other two must be in the house. Once inside, she faltered. There was no sign of them and no lights were on. The large, empty downstairs room was almost too dark to see anything. What light there was came through old glass in small paned windows, filtering green and aqueous into corners swallowed by lengthening shadows. The light switch was the old-fashioned kind, the sort you flick down. Nothing happened. Up, down, up again; still nothing. She jerked back from the wall as thunder ripped overhead like stiff fabric. The breaking storm must have caused a power cut. She held on to the back of a chair, waiting for her heart to stop racing, trying to make herself calm down.

Going upstairs, she called, 'Hugh? Will?'

Her voice sounded small, hollow, telling her the house was deserted, but still she went on looking: first in Hugh's room, then all the rooms, her dad's room, the bathroom, rooms with no possible reason for them to be in, her logic unravelling in the quiet of the house. But there was still no sign of them. Perhaps they were hiding, ready to jump out and frighten her, playing one of Hugh's stupid practical jokes. She paused outside Bethan's old room where Will had been working. Maybe they were in there.

She hesitated, noticing the number: *12a*. People use that instead of 13 for the numbers of houses and postal addresses, she thought. The metal knob slipped in her hand as she turned it. If the idea was to scare her, they were certainly succeeding.

There was no one in there, either. She sensed the room's emptiness as soon as she stepped into it, and stood listening. All was quiet – even the rain seemed to have stopped. Only the occasional drip fell from the eaves into the sudden absolute stillness. Then another sound crept in, a soft wheezing, like the building was breathing. There it was again, and again; regular, rhythmic. The creak and groan of rope and wood, followed by the whoosh of something heavy rushing through the air. The sound reaching out from her memory, going faster, and getting wilder, so her heart felt pushed up into her throat and she could hardly breathe.

Behind the wild seesawing there was something else: a strange kind of snuffling, like something sniffing out for her. The curtains flapped and snapped, blown into the room by a sudden squally gust from the window. Sally turned as the door slammed behind her. She ran to it, grabbing the handle, turning and pulling, panic obliterating what common sense she had left. It would not open. The thin sibilant chanting grew louder, amplified by the howl of the wind into a deep bellowing resonance, reverberating in her head until Sally thought her skull would explode. The pressure waves inside the room were building towards unbearable when suddenly the door opened and she was outside again.

She leaned against the wall in the corridor, sweat pouring down her back, breathing coming shallow. She had been turning the handle the wrong way. How stupid could you get? She didn't care where Will and Hugh were any more. She was leaving, right now. *They* could come and find *her*.

At the top of the stairs she stopped. The house below seemed unreal, its dimensions vague, the foot of the stairs, the room beyond, dissolving into shadow. She gripped the rail and took a few deep breaths, trying to get a hold of herself. She descended the staircase, keeping away from the creaking centre and staying close to the banister. It was important to be as quiet as possible. The house itself seemed to be listening for her, and instinct told her not to give away where she was.

Almost at the bottom, she stopped in mid-step. She thought the sound was another bout of thunder rolling, but this was different, low and rumbling, like a load of bricks falling. It was not coming from the sky outside, but from down in the cellar. It came again, and each burst was followed by a kind of gritty dragging, a muffled rattling. She put her foot on the next step and the plank bounced, snapping back, loud as gunshot. The other noise stopped. Then it was as if someone was listening, for her. Sally froze. Trapped. Unable to move up or down.

A hand caught her wrist. 'Sally?'

She bit back a scream, swallowing it down into her throat with a strangled murmur.

'What's the matter?' It was Will. She turned and threw her arms round him, trying to keep from sobbing.

'Gran said you'd come back here,' he said into her neck and hair. 'Hugh and I came to find you.'

Hugh cleared his throat, and stood back, embarrassed by their embrace.

'I came to look for you. I'm so glad . . .' Sally broke off. 'Listen.'

'To what?' Hugh frowned.

'That noise. There it is again.'

They all heard it this time. The slight scrape of metal on stone.

'There was something else before, like bricks tumbling . . .'

'Maybe it's the spook,' Hugh whispered back, 'or mice, or rats.'

'Rats don't use shovels.' Will dropped his voice to the lowest of murmurs. 'And ghosts don't demolish walls, they just glide through them. I think our friends have arrived, don't you?'

'How did they get in?' Hugh whispered. 'I saw your dad lock the door.'

'There are traps front and back for delivering barrels straight into the cellar.'

'Oh right. I didn't think of that.'

'Neither did I. They are in now: we'd better think what to do.'

'Perhaps we should get your dad, or the police,' Sally offered, not sure that they should risk any kind of confrontation themselves.

'And tell them what? By the time anyone got here, they would probably have cleared off. I want to see what they are up to.'

'And me,' Hugh agreed.

'OK. OK.' Outvoted, Sally nodded her agreement. 'We just look, though.'

'Yeah. Yeah, of course.' Will grinned, teeth white in the semi-dark. 'Right, then. This is what we do.'

22

The waiting was the hard part. They used the time to collect torches, check batteries, ready themselves. Gradually, tentatively at first, sounds from the cellar started up again. The work was continuing. The church clock struck one quarter-hour, then another, before Will declared it was safe to go down.

The cellar door was unlocked, despite what Hugh saw. Will turned the handle, trying to open it quietly, pausing when the hinges popped, holding the door up so it wouldn't scrape on the floor. Just inside, on the wall, was an old-fashioned fuse box. The lid hung open, its porcelain fuses pulled out. Finger on lips, Will tiptoed down the steps, beckoning the others to follow. They paused at the bottom, gathering in any sound and allowing their eyes to get used to the darkness. Pitch black thinned to greys – there was just enough light to see by. They were down here to investigate, not confront.

Will's trick seemed to have worked. Murmuring voices came from the far part of the cellar: two men talking, low but easy, like they had no fear of being discovered. Their talk was sporadic, punctuated by the ring of pick and hammer and the occasional rush of falling stone.

Will signalled to move forward. He aimed his torch at

the ground so they would not lose their footing, and kept one hand on the wall, feeling the way, as they moved from one room to another. Sally felt her breath come fast, stirring grit and dust from the stone as she passed.

They were approaching the last chamber, the largest space in the vast underground warren of the cellar. Will stopped, indicating for Hugh and Sally to do the same. He switched off his torch and flattened himself, cheek against stone, slowly working his body forward and around the arched entrance. One quick look and he was back.

The men were obviously not anticipating any interruption. A strong battery-operated light hung from a hook in the ceiling and a variety of tools lay strewn across the floor, each with *Jack Harding & Co.* stencilled on the handles. The men were using stolen tools, using Jack's own sledgehammers and crowbars to break down the wall. The bricks had been removed to leave an open stone archway. The sad pathetic rag remains of the cat had been kicked aside and lay scattered across the floor, strewn round the foot of the piled-up bricks.

The work continued out of sight, inside the tunnel. The ring of pickaxe on stone suggested they had met yet another barrier. Presently that noise ceased, replaced by grunting as if someone was attempting to move or lift a heavy object. Will strained to hear, trying to work out exactly what they could be doing: not lifting, more like pulling and shifting, first one way, then the other, the scrape of stone on stone. One block went and then another. The light swung slightly, as if stirred by a faint breeze. There was an odd smell, dry and musty, an exhalation of ancient air wafting through the cellar.

The stone-shifting stopped. Muttered conversation started up, too far away to be audible, but the tone – tense and heavy with suppressed excitement – was clear. They were breaking through into some kind of chamber outside the cellar perimeter.

Footsteps. One of the men was coming back. Will flattened himself against the wall. The light in the next room swung wildly and then the area was plunged into darkness. The three stayed frozen as the footsteps receded. One of the men had come to retrieve the light to illuminate the next phase of their work. The clash of metal on stone started again as they laboured to make the breach bigger.

'I'm going across,' Will whispered. 'You stay here.'

'No. Wait.' Sally held on to his arm.

Whatever she was going to say was drowned by a heavy fall of stone. There was the sound of scrambling and scrabbling. One of the men cried out. Dust and grit poured from the narrow tunnel entrance. Will and Sally jumped back, expecting the men to come running out, but they didn't. The sudden explosion of noise was followed by silence.

Will risked a look round the edge of the archway. The light was disappearing. The men had climbed through into somewhere else, leaving the cellar in darkness.

'I want to see where they've gone.' Will stepped forward. 'I'm going after them.'

'We're coming with you,' Hugh and Sally said together.

'OK. Stay behind me and close to the wall. If anything happens, the slightest sign they are on to us, then we are out of there. Agreed?'

They ducked into the entrance of the tunnel. A brief flash of the torch showed another wall, maybe fifteen metres forward. There was a jagged hole at the base; enough stone had been removed to allow a man to step through. Beyond this the bobbing light receded into darkness, moving away along some sort of passage.

Will went forward to the breach and risked another flash of the torch. It was a passage all right, maybe ten metres long and two wide. A bend took the end out of sight. He put out a hand. Walls, floor and ceiling all of stone. Big blocks, smooth, perfectly dressed, not the grey of the cellar behind – this was more like the red sandstone of the church. Maybe there was a connecting passageway between the two places. It was possible. He had heard rumours.

'Come on,' Hugh hissed in his ear. 'Are you going to stand there all day, or what?'

'All right. Let's go. But remember what I said.'

The short passage widened out into a five-sided stone chamber. The chapterhouse. This was where the Templars held their meetings, receptions, secret ceremonies. A narrow shelf, about knee-high, ran round the perimeter. It was divided into seats for each Knight and these were separated by ribbed stone pillars, extending upwards, bending over to meet and become the interlocking arches supporting the roof. In the centre of the stone floor was a structure Will did not expect, one he had not seen before, although he knew what it was. It was a reliquary. Thin stone tracery, intricately carved, as delicate as lace, formed a case to contain something beyond human price, something to be revered – something holy.

The two men were standing in front of the structure, studying it carefully. Will had to fight a desire to step forward, to reveal himself, in order to see what the reliquary contained, but he had to stay back from the entrance – concealed by shadows – at all costs.

One of the men shifted and Will held his breath, shocked by what he saw.

Two of the struts, slender as bone, lay shattered in pieces on the floor. The destruction was not recent; the stone showed no fresh discolouration. Two centuries of salts had oxidised to heal the jagged broken edges since Montegue Webster had smashed his way into this shrine within a shrine, but he had not gained what lay inside. He had staggered back, the vessels erupting in his head, blood flooding through his brain. By the time he had reached the outer passage, he would never see – or speak, or move – again.

Holt's hand-held light wavered over the surface of some

sort of casket, picking up the dark glitter of jewels, the soft gleam of precious metals, and offering glimpses of richly coloured enamel.

For one frozen moment, there was no movement. Then the taller of the two men lifted the heavy hammer he was carrying, smashed through the remaining carved stonework and reached in to grab the contents.

Maybe it was sixth sense, maybe some slight movement, but something alerted the men to the presence of others. They turned, Garvin holding the casket to his chest. It was almost too much for one man to carry. He was gasping slightly, muscles straining under the weight. Holt swung the light until it was blinding, full on the intruders, shining right in their eyes. He would brook no interference. He held them with his black stare and prepared to mount a psychic attack that would fry the brains inside their heads. Then he had a better idea. There was something here which could kill at a glance, make the seas boil, turn men to stone. He reached to open the jewel-encrusted gold-hinged doors. The thing in the casket would do the job for him.

Will tried to raise his own torch, but it fell from his hand, the thick white beam cartwheeling crazily, illuminating ceiling, wall, ceiling, as it rolled over and over. He tried to see how Sally and Hugh were doing, but could not move his head. All three were struck by a violent and sudden paralysis. They could only stare, helpless, unable even to blink, as the small doors began to swing open . . .

Will felt Hugh's hand clutch onto him, fingers with the strength of steel cutting into his wrist. Hugh held Sally, too. He was listening to words the other two could not hear; words that came clear and distinct straight into his right ear, rustling and settling in the quiet of his brain.

'Do not be afraid. Hold together and no harm will come to you.'

The voice was familiar, creaking like a rusty gate. It was the voice from the bookshop, and belonged to D. W. Ewart. The hand gripping him seemed to dig right through his shoulder, like pincers locking from one side to the other. The fingers were cold enough to make the flesh ache, hard and pointed, and the thumb in his back was rigid and jointed. He could feel every ridge, every edge. He did not want to see the owner. There was no cushion of flesh between these digits and his shoulder. The hand holding on to him was made out of bone.

Sally could not turn her head, but she too felt the presence of someone, something, standing behind her. The air around them was suddenly colder, carrying with it the stench of the grave. She glimpsed a black sleeve, felt rough serge on her cheek as an arm rose up beside her, pointing over her shoulder. Where there should have been a hand, a wrist, she caught the green-white gleam of articulated bone.

Holt had turned away from them, greedy for the first glimpse of the thing he had laboured so long to recover, trembling at the prospect of witnessing, first-hand, the havoc it could wreak. The casket began to shake. Garvin's grip on it was slackening. He looked up sharply at his companion and stared in disbelief as Garvin's face began to morph and contort, his mouth slackening, horror etching every line deeper, round eyes open wide in their sockets, the whites thick half-moons beneath dilated pupils. He was staring, transfixed, at something beyond Holt's shoulder − a sight terrible enough to make him lose his grasp on the casket.

Holt lurched forward, in a desperate effort to save it, but the casket began to fall. It crashed to the ground in seeming slow motion. Plaques of enamel and ivory, brittle with age, shattered. Ancient wood − fashioned from cedar felled in a different millennium − exploded, shivering into a thousand pieces and disintegrating into dust as it hit the hard stone floor.

The lead lining peeled back to reveal a round heavy object. Rotting cloth began to disintegrate on contact with the air, leaving gold thread webbed across skin the colour of drum-skins, as taut and leathery as bats' wings. Nose, jaw and cheek jutted, bone-sharp, through the stretched membranous covering. Wiry facial hair, badger-black and silver, clung in patches round thin liver-coloured lips peeled back from teeth exposed in a perpetual grin.

A thing of immense, incalculable evil lay on the floor before them: a diabolic creation containing, within the confines of the skull's bone cage, a functioning brain. It had spent centuries computing arcane mysteries. Occult knowledge, gathered like dew in the lost temples and hidden laboratories of the ancient Middle East, had been passed through countless distillations, to achieve the ultimate transmutation. Itself a proof of life everlasting, the head could alter the structure of matter: change the diamonds studded on the casket to smears of graphite; reduce the humans standing before it to their constituent components – little piles of iron and calcium and carbon; render the solid rock walls all around them back into so much sand.

The temperature in the chamber had been plunging. Sally clamped her jaw, only to realize that the small noise was somebody else's teeth chattering. There was another sound, a snuffling, sniffling. It was coming from the thing in front of them, as though it was activated by the proximity of human flesh. Then something else – a strange sibilant whispering, in some lost language not known to them, but all recognized the meaning. They felt the words of power, the weaving of intricate spells, and each one took a step forward. Holt stooped towards the head – desperate to save it, retrieve it, claim it for his own.

He stood, bent forward, hands held out, frozen in mid-gesture, unable to move, as slowly the eyes began to open. Lids peeled back over whites the decayed brown-yellow of rotten yolks. For a moment the eyes were sightless, then they rolled in the head to reveal blue-black irises, and deep in the centre of these, pupils, pinprick red, began to dilate. There, staring up at him, was the secret of the Templars – the legendary, magical head of Baphomet.

'Don't touch it! Don't go near it!' Hugh's voice rang out in warning, strengthened by some force outside himself. He held on to Will and Sally, his grip vice-like, drawing them back. Hugh saw armour glint in the darkness and a white-robed figure step from the shadows. Stephen de Banville, his mantle bearing the cross of the Templars, keeper of the treasure, guardian of this place – Hugh could see him, real as a living man, drawing his long sword as he strode towards the sickening thing that lay on the floor in front of them.

They saw a silver streak as the sword descended, and then the air was filled with the sharp thin reek of ozone as a ball of light, round, blue-bright, bolted across the chamber. A detonation followed, deeper than hearing. The earth shook. The room exploded, flashing white. Will grabbed hold of Hugh and Sally, and the three of them ran blind, guided only by an instinct to survive. Behind them the seat of the fire burnt with a fierce, chemical brightness. The choking smoke billowing out into the tunnel carried a gagging, noisome sweetness; a mixture of burnt flesh and corrupted incense.

Lightning fissured the night sky, thunder tore the air less than a heartbeat afterwards. A crooked fork zigzagged to the church, dancing, fizzing green and white, down the copper conductor. A tree – its canopy illuminated for a second, each branch and leaf clear and distinct – groaned under a hammer blow of 100,000 volts and split with a terrible rending crash.

They seemed to be standing in the very heart of the storm, but nothing would induce them to remain inside the pub a second longer than it took to leave it. They started off at a run, dodging instinctively, knowing to keep away from trees and to try to stay in the open. All the time it was as if someone, or something, was playing a kind of blindfold game with them, stabbing this way, then that way, trying to find them, to pick just the right spot.

The storm went on well into the night, not abating until some time in the early morning. Sally lay in the dark, safe in Edna's spare room, listening to a silence made absolute by the furious noise which had gone before it.

'What happened, Sally?' Bethan asked from the other bed.

'Nothing,' Sally replied, but it came out too pat, too fast. 'Go back to sleep.'

'Don't say that. I know it did.'

Bethan could be fobbed off – sometimes – but Sally sensed this was not one of those occasions. She knew things, could tell things. There was no point lying to her.

'You know those two men?' Sally began.

'The magician men?'

'Yes. They were looking for something special, hidden in

the cellar. We went to see what they wanted. That's all.'

'And they found the thing . . .' It was a statement not a question. 'What was it?'

'I'm not sure. I couldn't really see.' Sally had no trouble conjuring the scene, but it seemed unreal now, like part of a dream.

'What happened to it?'

'I don't know,' Sally replied. 'I really don't,' she added quickly, before Bethan could accuse her of lying. 'But the thing was very old. One of the men dropped the box it was in, and when he did that it crumbled away to dust.'

'What happened then?'

'Then we left.'

'The thing . . .' Bethan's voice came out of the darkness. 'It was nasty, wasn't it?'

Sally tried to keep the shudder out of her voice. 'Yes. It was.'

'And has it gone now?'

'Yes. I guess.'

'For ever?'

'Yes.'

Nothing could burn with that phosphorescent light and survive.

'Good.' Bethan yawned and turned over, preparing for sleep. 'The house will be all right now.'

23

In the morning people went out to look around, to marvel at the force of the storm. There were reports on the regional radio of structural damage, a car driven off the road, but no one seemed to have been hurt and there was nothing on the national news. The storm, although intense, seemed to have occurred only locally.

By the time Hugh and Will left Will's gran's house, the sun was out, steam rising from pavements drying in uneven patches.

'Look at that.' Will pointed to the paintwork and glass of the parked cars.

Hugh frowned, not sure what he was looking for. Then he saw. 'What is it?'

The rain, drying on the cars, had left a fine dust behind. Orangey yellow smears, like sandy tears, were all over the place, on any shiny surface.

'Dust sucked up into the stratosphere.'

'How did it get here?'

'Carried on the prevailing wind; then, when conditions are right, as in the storm last night, it gets dumped along with the rainfall.'

'Where does it come from, though?' Hugh asked. 'Originally, I mean?'

Will drew his forefinger across the bonnet of a car and examined the fine grains that came away.

'This,' he said, rubbing thumb against forefinger, feeling the grittiness, 'this has come all the way from the Sahara.'

'I want help this morning,' Jack told them when they got to the Saracen's Head. 'Down in the cellar.'

Will and Hugh exchanged looks and slowly followed Will's father down the cellar steps.

'Phew, dear!' Jack wrinkled his nose as he came to the bottom of the steps. A sweet reek was still heavy in the atmosphere. 'Funny old smell down here. Needs a proper airing – but it's not damp, that's the main thing.'

Jack carried on a monologue as he prodded about, checking on this and that. The two boys headed towards where they had been last night, retracing their route, threading through antechambers, until they came at last to the furthest part, the deepest recesses of the cellar.

They had no idea what to expect. Bricks piled chaotically, maybe even stonework fallen. They had not stayed around to see what happened to the two men, Holt and Garvin. Perhaps they would find them as well, bodies burnt, torn and broken as in the aftermath of some kind of explosion. What they actually found, what they actually discovered, stopped them dead in their tracks. The brickwork blocking the tunnel was back. All, apart from the one or two bricks Will's father had removed, were still intact.

'What's the matter?' They both jumped as Jack came up behind. 'You two look like you've seen a ghost.'

'No, Dad,' Will replied, blinking as though he could not quite believe his eyes. 'Quite the opposite, in fact.'

'Oh, my.' Edna put a hand to her mouth. 'Will you look at that? Good thing it wasn't near any houses.'

The old boundary oak at the end of Temple Field had been blasted in two. It looked like the tree was upside down: huge branches with their spreading canopy of leaves lay twisted and torn on the ground.

'What about that?' Bethan tugged at Edna's sleeve, and pointed. 'Looks like the field has got a hole in it.'

About twenty metres from the devastated tree, the rough pasture showed a burnt-out area, perfectly circular, about two metres across. The patch was black, the earth charred, but the grass round wasn't even scorched.

'Lightning strikes in the strangest of places. The tree I can understand, but that,' Edna shook her head, 'don't make any sense. Puts me in mind of something Lyn's dad told me about. Ball lightning he called it. He reckoned he'd seen it, different from normal lightning. Like a big ball of light falling from the sky, he said. He saw it roll along, then disappear down into the ground.'

'What was it, though?' Bethan asked.

'Some kind of strange weather phenomenon.' Edna shrugged her thin shoulders. 'Never seen it myself, but that doesn't mean it can't happen. Thank goodness it missed the

211

pub.' She glanced towards the old timber-framed building. 'Or you'd have no home to go to.'

Edna must have stepped into the Saracen's Head thousands of times over the years, and each time she entered – as worker or customer – she felt a dip in her spirits. All buildings have their own atmosphere. People said, 'The Saracen's is not a happy place,' and Edna had felt the truth of it. Today it felt different. Neither good nor bad. Instead there was a kind of emptiness, as if something had left and the building was waiting to see what would take its place.

Bethan felt it too. She could not say it in words, but her mood lightened. She was running around, carefree, laughing. Yesterday she would not go to the upstairs bathroom on her own, even in the daytime. Now she skipped off happily without asking anyone to go with her.

'I don't know what happened here last night, and I'm not going to ask,' Edna said as Bethan went up the stairs.

Sally opened her mouth and then closed it again, not sure what to say.

'Like I said, I won't pry,' the old lady went on. 'But last night, when you came back, it wasn't the storm that had scared you all, was it?'

Sally shook her head.

'I was worrying,' Edna confessed. 'I found that ouija board in Hugh's room, and I know what you young folks are like. I was worried you were dabbling with that, messing with things you don't understand. I was going to have words, but I thought I'd best wait for your dad. It was against my better judgement that I let you come up here last evening, in all that rain and everything, and when there was no sign of you for what seemed like hours . . .'

Edna paused, shaking her head, mouth pursed, brows drawn together. She suddenly looked her age as her face worked through the emotions she had experienced the night before.

'I kept telling myself, "They aren't little kids, and our Will's with them, and he's a sensible lad," but I was on the point of going to fetch my Jack when you came through the door.' The old lady's features creased with remembered relief, then she frowned again. 'But the look on your faces! It was as though the hounds of Hell were after you.'

'Edna. I . . .' Sally started to say, feeling bad at having caused so much distress, but the old lady waved her words away.

'No, hear me out. Like I said, I thought it was the storm – enough to scare the wits out of anyone – but now,' she looked at Sally, 'I'm not so sure. Whatever it was you did, it seems to have done the trick. But,' she gripped Sally's arm, 'you've got to promise not to do it again – not ever. Do you understand me?'

Sally nodded. 'I'm sorry, Edna,' she managed to say, 'We never meant to worry you. It was thoughtless.

213

And we'll never do anything like it again. I can absolutely promise—'

'Good, good.' Edna patted Sally's hand, and smiled. 'Don't take on now. It's over. If ever you want someone to talk to, I've a sympathetic ear. I've lived a long time, and I've seen things, been told things, that can't be explained in the ordinary way.'

Sally nodded again. It was a kind offer, and one she might take up. One day. But not yet. Sally would have to get what happened straight in her own head first before she could describe it to someone else.

'Dad's back.'

Bethan saw the car from her upstairs window. She came running down and rushed past Sally and Edna and out into the front yard.

The car was facing into the sun; it was hard to see who was inside. Sally expected just one door to open and her father to get out. When the other opened also, she thought it was probably the archaeologist, Clive Rowlands. The last person on earth she expected to step out of the passenger side of the car was her mother.

They all stood in a little group, not quite knowing what to do. Bethan ran to be scooped up and hugged, then Hugh came out with Will and Jack, and everybody was being introduced. Philip stood back, just smiling, not saying anything, as though he had gone off in a perfectly normal everyday way and come back with something special.

214

Edna and Janet liked each other immediately, Sally could tell, and that was a good, strong omen. Edna smiled, suddenly shy as she was introduced, but she liked the other woman's firm handshake and straight, honest look. Janet Goodman warmed to Edna's obvious no-nonsense kindness and thanked her for taking care of her children.

'This place needs a woman's touch, that's what I said all along.'

Edna took Janet off, showing her the house, and where everything lived, as though she was handing the keys to the chatelaine, the rightful keeper of the household.

'The holiday was a mistake,' Janet Goodman explained to Sally when they had a chance to speak alone. 'I knew it wasn't going to work as soon as I got off the plane. I didn't even bother to unpack. I needed time to think and then, when I was ready, I phoned to say I was coming back. I ended up having a long talk with your dad. He came to meet me at the airport,' she shrugged, 'and here I am.'

They were standing at the bottom of the stairs. She looked round. The ground floor was beginning to take form now, with the floors relaid and much of the plasterwork done.

'I think your father's right,' she added. 'I just couldn't see it before,' she smiled. 'I wasn't really looking, I suppose. Too much else on my mind to notice, but now I can see. This place really does have enormous potential.'

'Does that mean we are going to stay?' Sally asked, suddenly nervous, needing confirmation.

'Yes,' her mother answered. 'I rather think it does.'

'What about your job?'

'I've already resigned. Since Roger was my boss, I thought it politic. I've been thinking about going freelance, anyway, so where I live won't make any difference. Are you glad? Do you want to stay here?'

'Of course.'

'It wouldn't have anything to do with that rather handsome young man I met earlier, by any chance?'

Her mother's smile widened and Sally felt herself colouring. 'Of course not.'

Staying with Will wasn't the whole reason, but it did have something to do with it. She had been dreading having to say goodbye to him.

'I just want us to be together and be a family,' Bethan said simply. She had been at her mother's side all the time, small and quiet, like a shadow. She looked up at her now, eyes big and serious. 'And this place is as good as any. Have you seen the kittens?'

'No, Beth. I haven't.'

'Would you like to see them?'

'Yes, very much.'

'Come with me, then.' Bethan held out her hand. 'They live down in the stables. You have to be careful. Their mother is a bit fierce.'

Sally smiled, recognising the irony. Her own mother

turned from the door. 'I think we can make something good here.'

'Do you really believe that?'

'Absolutely.'

24

Holt and Garvin had disappeared from the village. 'Done a flit,' Edna said. 'Upped and went on the night of that storm.'

They were strangers, living in rented accommodation, so no one was really that bothered. Some thought they may have been the ones in the car driven off the road, but nobody knew for sure.

Will asked around but that was all he could find out. Gradually the two men, and what happened that night, slipped in priority. Sally and Hugh, in particular, had other matters on their minds.

Everyone in the Goodman family wanted things to work out right, but the first few days were difficult. They had to get used to the idea of living together again. It was hard to be natural with each other. Normal rhythms would develop and become established but, until that happened, it was as though there was a device in their midst that might go off any minute, activated by harsh words or bad behaviour. The strain on both Sally and Hugh was immense, enough to drive thoughts of the two men out of their heads.

Until Clive Rowlands arrived.

Rowlands was not most people's idea of a typical

archaeologist. He was slight, slim, with unusual pale hazel eyes in a thin oval face. His skin was dark, from working outside so much of the time, and he wore oversized fatigues, with combat boots laced almost to the knee. His flak jacket, open to the waist, showed bare arms and chest. His wrists were striped with woven bracelets and jangled with copper amulets. He wore a gold earring, and a thin beaded plait, with the rest of his long dark hair tied back in a ponytail.

He was down in the cellar making a preliminary assessment prior to excavation. The bricks blocking the entrance to the hidden chamber had been removed again. Rowlands picked a specimen out of the pile. 'You are right,' he said, looking up at Philip. 'I'd say this lot were eighteenth-century. Now then.' He stood and flashed a torch into the tunnel. 'Let's see what's in there.'

It was a week since Sally, Will and Hugh had been down there. Sometimes it seemed like none of it had really happened, that it was a collective dream they had been having, but now they would have to confront what had occurred and look at the proof of it. None of them had the slightest idea what they would find but they all felt a similar drying of the mouth, a closing up of the throat. It was all they could do to act casual and normal as Rowlands turned to them, asking: 'You kids coming, or what?'

Rowlands led the way forward, shining his light up the massive stone walls and along the vaulting.

'This is much older. Twelfth-century maybe. Fit the

Templar history. Good one, Phil.' He grinned up at Sally and Hugh's father. 'Could be interesting. You could be on to something.'

Sally's heart beat faster as they continued on towards the stone chamber she knew to be just round the corner. She glanced sideways at Will who was staring straight ahead, and then at Hugh. Sweat was standing in beads on the younger boy's upper lip and forehead.

'Are you all right?' she whispered.

Hugh nodded. 'What do you think he'll find?'

Sally shook her head.

'Your guess is as good as mine.'

Will nudged the other two into silence as the tunnel opened out. A faint sickly sweet smell still lingered. It was nothing like the stench of the week before, but it still hung strong enough to make each of them feel slightly nauseous. They paused for a moment, terrified of what might still be in there, not wanting to see it or go anywhere near it. Then Will took Sally's hand, as she groped for Hugh's, and together they steeled themselves to enter.

Clive let out a low whistle. 'Looks like the Templars' chapterhouse all right.'

The chamber appeared to be empty, the walls a stone skin surrounding the shattered reliquary. There was nothing on the floor except a few scattered grave slabs. Sally felt relief sweeping through her. Holt and Garvin must have got out.

Philip directed his light on to the reliquary, playing the beam across the carved stone tracery. He was just about to go and investigate further when Clive held him back.

'Careful, Phil. There's something by your foot.'

'Well, I'll be . . .'

Clive aimed his torch beam at a sliver of carved wood. A gem gleamed dull-red in the white light, but it was not that which had caused the exclamation, the sharp intake of breath.

'What?'

Philip Goodman crouched down to see what his colleague was examining so carefully. At the centre of the shattered casket lay a small pile of white powder, as fine as flour. Clive Rowlands touched it lightly, testing the texture between thumb and forefinger. Then he turned his attention to a thick oily substance adhering to the shards of wood.

'What is it?' Philip asked.

'I'm not sure . . .' Clive shone his torch round the find. 'This is obviously a reliquary of some kind. And this,' he indicated the coarse white powder and sticky substance, 'must be what it contained.'

'What do you think this is?' Philip extended an index finger to the treacly stuff. It felt tarry and unpleasant.

'I don't know.'

'What do you think happened here?'

Clive Rowlands stood up. 'I have no idea.' He shrugged

his shoulders, thoroughly at a loss. 'But I'd say the white powder is bone, probably human.'

'Hey now, hang on a minute.' Philip sat back on his haunches. 'It would take a phenomenal temperature to obtain that degree of calcination. Even modern crematoria can't reduce bone to powder.'

'I know. That's what's strange about it. It *looks* like . . .'

'Looks like what?'

The young archaeologist gave a nervous laugh. 'You'd just scoff. Come on, let's take some samples and get them off to the lab. We can argue about it when the results come out.' He reached in his pocket and pulled out some plastic wallets. 'Any of you three want to help?'

'No thanks.' Hugh spoke for all of them.

'Kids!' Philip shook his head at the retreating footsteps. 'And I thought he was interested . . .'

Laboratory tests confirmed Clive Rowlands' opinion. The remains found within the shattered casket were human, but the report did not explain what might have happened to produce such peculiar changes to bone and flesh.

Clive had his own theory: spontaneous combustion of the casket contents caused by the action of a so-far-unexplained phenomenon. Spontaneous combustion is often associated with electrical activity, particularly ball lightning, and can result in organic matter bursting into flames, burning up in a fire which is at once intense and highly localised.

Philip, of course, dismissed this as fanciful nonsense,

X-Files baloney, but they did not fall out in a major way about it. The excavations went ahead through the summer, providing Philip with the information he needed to chart the history of the Saracen's Head from Templar preceptory to family dwelling.

Summer turned into autumn. The car park around the pub had gone, been dug up, a nascent garden planted. Janet was turning the Saracen's Head into a home of some elegance and, so far, a happy one. The children settled into new schools. Sally and Will continued to be an item. Hugh found friends in the village and had joined the local football team. Bethan's kittens had turned from roly-poly balls of fur into four young cats – all with names and promoted from strays to family pets.

Through the autumn, Philip continued his research. He read and reread Montegue Webster's journals. He combed the records, went through the archives and interviewed local people, collecting all the stories he could find.

He planned to write his book through the winter, and the first day of December found him sitting in his study wondering exactly how to begin. He turned on his computer, and started to type the first sentence. What appeared on the screen rather surprised him.

Despite my natural scepticism, I have come to realize that there are episodes that defy any rational explanation in the long and strange history of the Saracen's Head . . .